BREAKDOWN

JACK BONAFIDE BOOK THREE

JORDAN VEZINA

MOUNTAIN WOLF PRESS

AUTHOR'S NOTE

If you did not read the free short story "Ex-Agents" after **Jack Bonafide Book 2: High Tension** please download it using the link below. It contains necessary information that contributes to the story you are about to read.

https://dl.bookfunnel.com/qyvfchet85

**The Home of David Kelvin
Washington D.C.
March 20, 1981**

Former Attorney General of the United States David Kelvin was a man of great experience. He had seen many things during the Second World War and in his years of public service that he thought should have prepared him for anything.

However, all of those years and all of those experiences could not possibly have prepared him for this.

"I'm... I'm not sure how to respond," he said.

"Have another drink," Arkady Radovich replied as he walked to the wet bar in Kelvin's study. "I often find alcohol helps in situations such as this."

Kelvin stared blankly at Arkady for a moment and then turned back to Richard Feldman, a man he now knew to be Tolya Rodin.

It was true: Kelvin had been elbow-deep in a lot of dirty deeds—particularly of late—but he now found himself playing at a whole different level. This man, this noted financier and close personal friend to the President of the United States, was a *Soviet spy?*

Then, with this new information at hand, Kelvin's mind immediately began to shift away from how this scenario might negatively impact him to how he might use the knowledge to his benefit.

The President's close friend is a Soviet spy, Kelvin thought to himself. *That has to be worth something. Perhaps even the position of Vice President, if I play my cards right. And after that? Who knows.*

"Here," Arkady said, offering the Old Fashioned to Kelvin.

"Thank you," Kelvin replied as he accepted the drink. He downed half of it in one shot.

"So, now you know," Tolya said quietly from his position behind Kelvin's desk. He folded his hands on the blotter. "You're in the big game now."

"You'll excuse me for asking," Kelvin said, "but why?"

"What do you mean?" Tolya asked.

"Well, I'm not trying to talk myself out of a job here, but what do I bring to the table? At the moment, I'm what one might call 'unemployed.'"

Tolya looked to the calendar on the wall.

"Are you saying you have given up your aspirations to the governorship of New York?"

"New York?" Kelvin laughed. "I think that ship has sailed. Caldwell is a goddamn hero now after that neo-Nazi lunatic shot him and he survived, and while I may have saved some face, everyone in the Republican Party knows I was thrown out on my ass! I won't even make it past the primaries, much less reach the general election."

"What *if* you could, though?" Tolya asked. "What if, at the zero hour, Caldwell went away, and you were the only one remaining to step in and rescue the future of the Republican Party in the State of New York?"

"Have you got any unicorns you can sell me while you're at it?" Kelvin scoffed.

"Careful," Arkady admonished him.

Kelvin turned to the large man and felt a jolt of fear. He had let his mouth run away with him again.

"Look," Kelvin said, holding up his hands in a placating gesture. "You have to understand that you're throwing a lot at me. Okay. If you could make all of that happen; what would you want from me in return?"

"A favor," Tolya said.

"A favor?" Kelvin parroted.

"Yes. To be paid at a time of my choosing."

"Why do I feel like I'm not going to like this favor?" Kelvin surmised.

"They still have the logbook," Arkady stepped in. "At this point, we must be ready for potential blowback if someone connects the dots and discovers just who Tolya Rodin really is."

Kelvin turned back to Tolya Rodin, who, up until that point, he had known only as Richard Feldman.

"I think I deserve to know," Kelvin said pointedly.

"Know what?" Tolya demurred.

"What you're planning!" Kelvin insisted. "If I'm going to be hip-deep in this shit, I think I deserve to know what kind of shit it is."

"You do not want to know," Tolya said. "That, I promise you."

"I think I should be the judge of that."

Tolya drummed his fingers on the desk for a moment and then nodded his head.

"I'm going to kill the President."

The air was sucked out of the room. Kelvin felt his fingers go cold. He had really done it this time. He felt Arkady's hand on his shoulder.

"You should learn to heed wise counsel when it's given to you," Arkady said, the chill in his voice obvious. "Now you know, my friend, just what kind of shit you're in."

"More importantly," Tolya said, "there is no way out now."

"But... why would you kill him? To what purpose?" Kelvin stammered. "I thought he was your friend?"

"My *friend?*" Tolya laughed. "He is as much my friend as the cat is a friend to the mouse. He is just one more tool, but a tool that I have needed in a very specific position and in a very specific frame of mind. He has now stepped out of that role. This is something I cannot abide."

"But—but I don't understand," Kelvin said, stepping forward and shaking off Arkady's hand. "I thought you were done with the KGB?"

"This has nothing to do with the KGB or Mother Russia." Tolya opened a desk drawer and retrieved one of Kelvin's Cuban cigars. He went about the ritual of snipping off the end and then lit it. He puffed with great satisfaction, obviously savoring the suspense. "Do you know how much I am worth, Mister Kelvin?"

"I—no, I don't."

"It starts with a *B*," Tolya said. "And I plan for it to stay that way. This means I cannot have an American president upsetting world markets and launching investigations into corporations. It would be bad for business."

"What makes you think all of that will happen?"

"I am a student of history, Mister Kelvin. I know that it will happen, because it *has* all happened before—and, as I said, this I cannot allow."

"How will you do it?"

"Is that really a question you want to be asking, Mister Kelvin? Is it truly your wish to sink yourself deeper into this 'shit,' as you call it?"

"I figure I'm fully in as it is," Kelvin answered. "I might as well know what it tastes like, too."

Tolya laughed at this. He was beginning to develop a strange fondness for the former attorney general.

"It's a stroke of genius, really. In fact, you were the one who started the process."

"*Me?*" Kelvin asked. "What the hell did I have to do with it?"

"You had Mister Bonafide committed to a psychiatric facility," Tolya said. "Correct?"

Kelvin was taken aback. He had thought that information was a secret. Had Braxton told someone?

"It had to be done!" Kelvin countered. "That fucking redneck kept getting in the way! If—if it weren't for him, that damn logbook would have been burned long ago! In fact, you should be thanking me!"

"But I am," Tolya said with a smile. "After a fashion. You see, without knowing it, you put Mister Bonafide right where I needed him to be. Yet one thing still troubles me."

"And what would that be?"

"Was it spite, Mister Kelvin? The reason you had Mister Bonafide committed?"

"I told you—he kept getting in the way," Kelvin insisted. "He was on to you, I can assure you of that."

"Hmm. Even if he was, I doubt much would have come of it," Tolya said as he took another puff from the fine Cuban cigar.

"Those are expensive, you know," Kelvin said, sounding minorly annoyed.

Tolya laughed, almost choking on the mix of humor and smoke.

"You are indeed a strange man, Mister Kelvin. So obsessed with the pedigree of the dog that you don't notice when he's chewing your leg off."

Kelvin cocked his head to the side in thought.

"Wait," he said. "You said that I put Jack Bonafide right where you needed him." He paused for a moment. "For what?"

Tolya's gaze became cold.

"Why... to kill the President, of course."

A silence overtook the room.

"And how are you going to do that?" Kelvin asked.

"I assume you remember MK Ultra?" Tolya said. "The CIA's mind control experiment."

"Of course," Kelvin replied. "But that program was retired."

"Yet still it lives on. We have at our disposal one of the brilliant minds behind that program."

"And he's going to turn Bonafide against his own country?" Kelvin scoffed. "Good luck with that."

"Luck is the province of fools and Democrats," Tolya said. "We have a plan."

"Did you bring the information we requested?" Arkady asked.

Now Kelvin understood why they had wanted Jack Bonafide's full dossier.

"Yes," Kelvin replied.

He reached into his jacket, retrieved four manila folders, and then handed the first to Arkady.

The tall Russian took it and turned the pages.

"Delta Force," Arkady said. He was privately disappointed that none of his sources, acquired through Tolya Rodin's own connections, had uncovered that piece of information. "That changes things."

"What of the others?" Tolya asked, indicating the folders Kelvin still held. "Anything worth noting?"

"Scarn and Finster are the usual story; nothing really interesting there," Kelvin said as he set the folders down on the desk. "Carrie Davidson, though —her file makes for some *interesting* bedtime reading."

Tolya picked up the folder labeled with Carrie Davidson's name and began flipping through the pages. He stopped at one page and shook his head.

"In the Soviet Union," he said, "we did things like this to our own agents. I, myself, was on the receiving end of such treatment. The difference is that we knew it was happening."

"If anyone finds out I got my hands on that folder, it'll mean serious prison time for me," Kelvin said. "That's Coal Chamber material."

"Coal Chamber?" Arkady asked, his curiosity sufficiently piqued.

"Darker than dark," Kelvin said. "They don't even answer to the Director of the CIA—unless he's stupid enough to open the sealed files."

"Then how do you know about them?" Tolya asked.

"Money talks and bullshit walks," Kelvin said. "I still have enough of it that I can buy my way to the most secret of information. Money, not bullshit."

"And I expect you will want to be reimbursed?" Tolya ventured.

"I think I deserve to be."

"And the governorship of New York is not enough for you?"

"I can't buy a yacht with a promise," Kelvin replied.

"Fair enough," Tolya agreed.

David Kelvin sat down in his chair and let out a long sigh. Tolya Rodin and Arkady Radovich had left, and he was alone again. He checked his watch. In a little more than twenty-four hours, he would need to make a phone call that would undoubtedly change the world.

He would still play Tolya Rodin's game because while what he was planning would change the world, it wasn't going to end it. America would endure.

It was just a matter of what that America would look like.

The Office of the Director
CIA Headquarters
Langley, Virginia
March 20, 1981

Mike Tresham stood in his office and surveyed his kingdom. Specifically, it was a kingdom of paperwork. Piles and piles of it sat atop his desk, with no end in sight.

The door opened behind him, and he turned to see Eleanor Babbitt enter with another armful of folders. Eleanor had served as Administrative Assistant to the Director for as long as anyone could remember, Mike included. She was a prim and proper woman in her mid-sixties, and despite her expert skills at brewing a cup of tea and organizing vast piles of paperwork, she was also a proficient combat marksman and had proven on more than one occasion that she was not to be taken lightly.

Eleanor crossed the room and dropped the sealed folders onto Tresham's desk.

"These are the sealed folders," she said.

Tresham nodded. "I can see that," he said.

Eleanor handed Tresham a clipboard with a form on it, the carbon copies stacked beneath.

"To be signed in triplicate," she said. "Please acknowledge receipt of the sealed folders so that they can go back in the safe."

Tresham raised an eyebrow.

"We're not going to confirm the contents?"

Eleanor let out a sigh.

"Mister Director, you'll excuse my bluntness, but I am no longer a young woman. I've done this dance with four other directors before you. It is best for the Agency, and—if you don't mind me saying so—for you, if those folders stay sealed."

"Wait a minute. Are you trying to tell me that there are ongoing operations that *no one* knows about, including the Director of the CIA?"

"They're not all operations," Eleanor said. "Some are deep cover identities. But, yes, there are a number of clandestine operations."

"Look, Eleanor, I appreciate your counsel, but I'm opening these folders."

Eleanor looked at the dozen folders she held.

"Are you sure?"

"I can't even believe I'm having this conversation! *Yes.* I'm sure."

"Fine," Eleanor said, and she set the stack down on Tresham's desk.

She turned and handed him the first file. Mike looked at the seal on the envelope.

"Jesus Christ! This thing has been sealed since *sixty-eight*? What the hell is going on around here?"

"This is the CIA, Mister Director," Eleanor said with a smile. "We have the odd secret here and there."

Mike ripped open the folder and noticed that Eleanor visibly winced. He would need to find out just how deep this all went, and what she really knew. He pulled out a sheath of documents and quickly read them over.

"What in the hell is the Coal Chamber?"

"Oh, yes. That one. Daniel Flynn." Eleanor

pursed her lips and then nodded. "Yes, you're going to want to seal that one back up."

"The hell I will!" Tresham scowled as he began reading through the documents. "We set up a wet works program in sixty-eight and then just put it on auto-pilot?"

"Well, there's a little more to it than that. I assume you remember MK Ultra?"

"I wish I could forget," Tresham said, recalling the mind control experiments the CIA had performed in the late sixties. "All that brainwashing bullshit was a colossal waste of time."

"Well, it was, and it wasn't," Eleanor said. "The mind control part didn't go quite as expected, but it wasn't a complete failure. It helped the Agency to figure out a few things."

"Such as?"

"I'm not privy," Eleanor replied. "And I doubt you'll find much about it in there."

"So, where would I find out about this?"

Eleanor sighed.

"If you really must, I imagine you would have to bring Daniel Flynn in from the cold."

"Who the hell is this guy?"

"*She*," Eleanor said, "was a bit of a problem child.

Until she got the right project. Now she works on the periphery of our active operations."

"Well, I want to talk to her."

"Fine," Eleanor replied curtly. "But I'm going to be putting in my retirement papers."

"Why on earth now?"

"Because you've just lifted the lid on the proverbial Pandora's box," Eleanor said. "And I don't want to be around when the bitch goes nuclear."

CHAPTER 1

The Apartment of Clark Finster
Washington D.C.
March 20, 1981

"You LOOK LIKE SHIT," Assistant Director of the CIA Michael Scarn said as he handed Clark a styrofoam cup full of hot black coffee. "And you shouldn't answer your door without your weapon. We're still working under active protocols. Even if you aren't."

Clark rubbed his eyes and took the cup of coffee. He turned and walked back into the apartment without a word. Scarn followed him and looked around the small two-bedroom dwelling.

"*Jesus*, Clark. How many serial killers live here?" Scarn asked, only half-joking.

He wasn't far off. The place was a mess, and the walls were covered with a vast array of maps, photographs, and intelligence papers.

"Just the one," Clark said lazily as he drank from the coffee cup and returned to a large map of the D.C. Metro area that covered most of the south wall of his living room.

"What do you see there?" Scarn ventured, gesturing to the map. It was full of pins linked together by different strands of string.

"Something," Clark said. "I just can't see the whole picture yet."

"It's been nearly three weeks," Scarn said quietly.

"I know how long it's been!" Clark snapped, before immediately feeling ashamed by his response. "Sorry. It's probably also how long it's been since I got a full night's sleep."

The CIA had stopped looking for Jack Bonafide. To Clark, that was a mistake; they had stopped looking quite a bit too soon for his taste. They had probably put a total of seventy-two hard hours into the search for a man who had basically just saved the country before relegating it to a "second tier" tasking, which was not good. That was the same tier where the hunt for the Lindbergh baby had been filed.

"Is there anything I can do?" Scarn asked. "I know that you said you would work best alone on this, but could you use anything in the way of resources?"

"Thanks for the coffee," Clark said.

"Look... there's something else," Scarn said.

Clark turned to him.

"What?"

"Tresham wants to know when you're coming back."

"When I find Jack," Clark said flatly. "We come back together, or not at all."

Scarn nodded. He understood what was happening. Clark Finster wasn't a man who had many friends, which Scarn understood all too well, because he, too, didn't have many friends. In fact, if he was being honest about it, he didn't have *any*. That was just the way it had always been. It seemed as though he just wasn't a man that people liked. When he was younger, it had been a matter of some consternation to him, but as he grew older, he became somehow comfortable with it. It almost felt as if there was a certain degree of nobility in being lonely.

Jack was Clark's friend. Maybe his first true

friend. If Scarn had a friend like that, how far would he go to try and help him?

"Okay," Scarn said, taking off his suit jacket and tossing it over a chair. "What have we got so far?"

Clark stared at Scarn for a moment and then turned back to the large map on the wall.

"March 3rd, Jack disappears. Without a *fucking* trace. His truck is found outside the apartment the CIA set up for him, but the doors aren't locked."

"Which suggests he was taken," Scarn surmised.

"Exactly. A man like Jack doesn't just leave doors unlocked. But there were no blood droplets, no skid marks, and no sign of a struggle. No witnesses. Who can take a man like that without leaving a trace?"

Scarn thought about it for a moment and then shrugged.

"Us, I guess," he said.

"Or someone like us."

"Freelancers? Former Agency? Is there anyone out there like that for hire?"

"No," Clark said. "We keep a pretty close eye on all of them. So, we then extrapolate out from that. It's not Agency, but it could be Special Operations. So, we start running through all of them."

Clark walked over to another board with roughly

thirty photos pinned to it. Most were military identification photos.

"These guys? Scarn asked.

"Those are all of the freelancers with spec ops backgrounds operating in the Metro Area."

Scarn turned to Clark.

"We have this information," he said. "The Agency does."

"That's right."

"But you shouldn't."

"Right again," Clark said.

"Your credentials were revoked when you took leave."

The implications were obvious. Clark had illegally hacked into the CIA database to get the information he needed.

"Jesus Christ, Scarn! Do we have to do this fucking dance right now?"

Michael Scarn paused for a moment and then shook his head. He didn't need to know how Clark had accessed the CIA database. It wasn't important.

"No. So, what has this told you?"

"I pulled three names from this group that don't add up. Two are former SEALs with pretty clean records. One guy got picked up on a drunk and disorderly charge last year, but that's not enough to think he's crooked enough to try to kidnap Jack, or even be able to." Clark turned to another photo. "Then there's this guy."

Scarn walked to the board and looked at the photo pulled from British Intelligence.

"Rory Braxton," Clark said.

"What's his story?"

"Former British SAS, then did a lateral move to MI6."

"Heavy hitter," Scarn said.

"Seems like it. Then he just dropped off the radar and resurfaced here in seventy-nine."

"Doing what?"

Clark turned to Scarn.

"As Kelvin's driver."

"You're shitting me!" Scarn blurted.

"I shit you not."

"There's no way that's a coincidence."

"My thoughts exactly. Which is why we could do with asking a few pertinent questions. Fortunately, we have leverage," Clark said.

"How so?" Scarn asked.

"Braxton's an illegal. No papers."

"Interesting." Scarn thought for a moment. "So, where does that leave us?"

"I have a name," Clark said, "but that's it. I can't

approach Braxton in any official capacity. And I damn sure can't walk up to Kelvin and start questioning *him*, even if I was still on duty. He may not be the A.G. anymore, but he still has plenty of friends in high places."

"You're right; you can't," Scarn said. "But *I* can."

"You'd do that?" Clark asked.

"It's not just about Jack," Scarn said. "We know that Kelvin was linked to that logbook, and now it looks like you may have found a connection between him and whoever took our man."

"So, what are we going to do about it?"

"I think we need to pay Mister Kelvin a little visit. It's one thing for an analyst on leave to drop in on him, but a visit from the Assistant Director of the CIA is another matter entirely."

Saint Elizabeth's Mental Hospital
The Office of Doctor Noah Barrister
March 20, 1981

"Are the lights bothering your eyes?" Doctor Barrister asked.

He leaned forward across his desk and pushed his glasses back up the bridge of his nose. He was a tall man, standing at six foot four, but as he was never a fan of exercise he only weighed one hundred and sixty pounds.

The office was meticulously decorated, with Doctor Noah Barrister's Harvard medical degree prominently displayed on the wall behind him and backlit by a small light mounted above it to ensure it would not go unseen. Alongside it were various accolades from numerous medical institutions, as well as those from the United States government and, specifically, the Department of Defense.

"They're... fine," Jack said slowly.

Jack Bonafide was still having trouble forming complete sentences. He guessed he had been this way for nearly three weeks, but he couldn't be certain, as he was also having trouble tracking time. He continued to work his hands inside the straitjacket, looking for a weak point; looking for anything he could exploit when the opportunity presented itself.

He was also attempting to track the dosages of Thorazine he was being administered. The doses came every twelve hours, and the sadistic sons of bitches never missed a dose. Except for when they hit him with adrenaline, and then everything turned upside down. For a few minutes, at least.

Jack stared at the doctor, but despite his response to Noah Barrister's question, the lights *did* bother his eyes. In fact, they bothered the hell out of him, but there was no way he was going to say anything about it.

Try as he might, Jack could not seem to remember much about how he had arrived at the hospital or his life before doing so. There were flashes of memory, almost like scenes out of some horror movie, but nothing that he could really grab on to and call his own. He remembered the Army, Delta Force, and even the CIA, but those memories were all a jumble. Timelines mixed in with each other and even overlapped.

That wasn't the worst of it. The worst was that his concussion symptoms were back, and they were back with a vengeance. The ringing in his ears was persistent, and even though he couldn't get his hands free, he could feel that they were trembling beneath the straight jacket.

"How many?" Doctor Barrister asked.

"How many what?" Jack replied.

"Lights," the doctor replied. "How many lights do you see?"

Shit, Jack thought to himself. *Not this again.*

He did not respond.

Doctor Barrister leaned to the side and worked a dial. The lights became brighter.

"How many lights do you see, Mister Bonafide?"

"Two," Jack said.

He knew there was no point in stonewalling. The lights would just get brighter, and then the recording of the crying baby would start.

"No, Mister Bonafide. I'm sorry," Doctor Barrister said as he turned the lights up again. "There are three lights."

Jack tucked his chin and looked at the floor. He knew the game by now. Whoever this guy was, he just wanted him to talk. As long as Jack gave some form of answer, things wouldn't get too crazy. At least, not for a while.

But while he was willing to give a basic answer, there was no way in hell he was going to say that there were three lights when he knew damn well there were only two.

Jack shuffled down the hallway. His back hurt. They only let him out of the straitjacket for three reasons. To eat, to shit, and to fight. Otherwise, he even slept in the damn thing. When they did take it off, there were usually three orderlies standing around him with cattle prods, and the few times he had tried to make a break for it, he was out before he even knew what had hit him.

So, he did the same thing he had done during prisoner of war training with Delta. He just kept counting backward from one hundred. Over, and over, and over. This exercise alone would have been enough to drive anyone else insane all on its own, but for Jack, it was the only thing keeping him from going over the edge. The countdown was something he had control over. It was predictable. It had an end point.

Whatever this place was— *wherever* it was—it was some kind of asylum. It had to be. He had seen enough people who looked like psychiatric patients to know this, but they were strangely integrated with other folks like him, who seemed mostly normal but had been drugged to the gills.

Then there were the others. They were the ones that Jack was put up against. So far, it had only happened three times, but each time was the same. The jacket would come off, the orderlies would hit him with the adrenaline, and then it was time to get it on.

Afterward, when he was the only one left standing, he would get a steak. That was the really weird part. They would take him to a quiet room and serve him steak and Lone Star Beer.

He imagined it was supposed to be some sort of reward for having just killed a man. Around here, it seemed as though they took a pound of flesh quite literally.

"Your quarters," Foster said, as he turned a key in the lock to Jack's room. "Sorry the maid hasn't been around."

Jack would have smiled, but he knew he was drooling on himself. Foster was a good one; at least, as much as any of the orderlies could be. During what passed for conversation between the two of them, Jack had learned that Foster had played fullback at LSU but had failed medical school.

There was something more about the man, though. Something he wasn't letting on about. Jack knew the man was more than just an orderly. Perhaps ex-military. The other orderlies had the same sort of air about them. They were more than just medical personnel.

Jack shuffled into the room and sat down on the edge of his cot. He looked at Foster.

"Can I... get this... off?" He asked slowly, indicating the straitjacket.

Foster looked uncomfortable.

"It's coming off in about fifteen minutes."

"Shit," Jack said.

"Look, Jack," Foster said. "They're probably going to be bringing them in faster now, maybe every few days instead of one or two a week. Maybe even more than that."

"Why?"

"Well... because you're good at it. Everyone else is either killed or gets too banged up, after a while, to keep fighting. You're different. Like I said, you're *good* at it."

For just a moment, Jack thought about telling Foster who he was, to see if he could get a message to the outside, but that would be a violation of the first rule of being a prisoner of war. *Do not give the enemy any information you don't have to.* The truth was, he didn't really know this man. He didn't know for sure that he wouldn't turn right around and tell Doctor Barrister everything he said.

"Maybe I should have been an... accountant," Jack drawled.

Foster laughed and then took a knee in front of Jack.

"Jack, what you're doing here is important. These are bad guys you're going up against. Cartel, Cosa Nostra, kidnappers, murderers. The authorities can't touch them, but we can. What you're doing here— what Doctor Barrister is doing here—is important." Foster seemed as though he was searching for the right words. "A man like you, with your condition and your skills—what would you be doing on the outside?"

"My... *condition?*" Jack asked.

"Schizophrenia, Jack. Like your Uncle John, right? I read about it; about what happened in Texas in the fifties. It's not fair, I get it, but you've got the same thing he had. At least this way you can use it for some good."

Jack stared blankly at Foster. Someone had devised quite a narrative. Most likely, they had erased his past and replaced it with this fiction. Yes, it was true his Uncle John had gone on a notorious killing spree in South Texas back in the fifties, but that didn't have a damn thing to do with him.

Not that it mattered much. This Doctor Barrister had obviously discovered Jack's family history, and now he was using it to keep him under wraps.

. . .

Doctor Barrister walked through the long hallway of the first sub-basement and stopped in the semi-darkness to get his bearings. Prior to his need to use these tunnels as meeting spots, he had never ventured beneath the hospital. He considered it a very real possibility that he could become lost in these tunnels, never to be seen again.

"I thought you had gotten lost," a voice called out from the darkness.

Noah Barrister jumped and then narrowed his eyes to try and make out the figure that was several feet away from him. The man had a Russian accent.

"You're his man?" Noah asked.

"I am my own man," Arkady Radovich replied. "But if you are asking whether I work for Mister Feldman, I will tell you that I do."

"Either way," Noah said dismissively, "I was told you have information for me?"

Arkady stared at the man for a moment and then reached into his jacket, retrieving a folder and handing it to him.

"He won't be easy to break. Not like you thought he'd be," Arkady said.

Noah thumbed through the pages for a moment and then looked up at Arkady with wide eyes.

"Jesus, man! He was in Delta Force?" Noah exclaimed.

"Yes."

"Why in the hell did you wait until now to tell me this?"

"We only just found out. We knew he was CIA and that he was a man of some resource, but we did not know about the Special Forces background."

"I worked with these men," Noah said, shaking his head. "In the beginning, when the unit was founded. I must have crossed paths with him, but I don't remember."

"Can you still turn him?" Arkady asked.

Noah thought about it for a moment.

"I think I can."

"You *think*?" Arkady mocked.

"What the hell do you want from me?" Noah nearly shouted. "We're in uncharted waters here. All I can promise is that I'll do my best."

Jack stood in front of the doorway as Foster worked the buckles of his straitjacket, gradually loosening them until he was able to slip the entire jacket off.

Jack could feel his arms relax, and he cracked his knuckles. He looked around at the orderlies who surrounded him with their cattle prods.

"Don't even fucking *think* about it," one of them snarled.

Jack had heard the other men call this one Grunewald. He was a big man of German heritage, who looked like he'd taken one too many blows to the head. He had also derived a little too much pleasure in hitting Jack with the cattle prod a couple of times before.

"Wouldn't dream of it," Jack said. "Just... loosening up."

"Smart ass," Grunewald said and then smiled. "Maybe we should let you go this round without your little pick-me-up?"

That would be the worst-case scenario. Jack was usually doped up on Thorazine when going up against whoever would be standing in the padded room he was about to walk into.

"Shut up, Grunewald," Foster snapped. "Everyone knows you're full of shit. Doctor Barrister's orders are clear."

Grunewald stepped to Foster, and the two went nose-to-nose. Jack did the mental calculations. Was this his time? Could he make a play here; use this conflict to make a break for it? No, it was too risky. He was being impatient, and he knew it. He slowly let out a breath and calmed himself.

Grunewald locked eyes with Foster for a moment and then slowly broke into a smile.

"Fuck you, redneck," Grunewald spat and then took a step back. "Fine. Whatever."

Foster ignored the insult and pulled a syringe from his pocket.

"You ready?" Foster asked.

"Yeah," Jack said. "I'm ready."

Foster turned to another orderly.

"Open it!"

The orderly opened the door and Jack looked into the large padded room. Inside stood a man with long black hair, his arms covered with prison tattoos. He wore a long handlebar mustache and had a scar across his face.

"He's cartel, Jack," Foster said. "His name's Sobrante. He's the real deal. He killed a dozen women in Rosales; cut their heads off. DEA extracted him on a drugs charge, but he would have walked."

Jack turned to Foster.

"And *I'm* the schizophrenic?" Jack asked.

Then Jack saw it. There was doubt in Foster's

eyes, but not enough to stop him from hitting Jack with the adrenaline, shoving him through the door, and slamming it shut.

The room was silent. It was like the air had been sucked out of it.

Jack could feel himself starting to come back to life. His heart rate was increasing, and every hair on his body stood on end. He wasn't getting the full effect of the adrenaline, mostly because it was only intended to counter the Thorazine, but he was getting enough that it was noticeable.

The man across the room smiled. That wasn't a good sign.

"I guess they want me to kill you," Sobrante said. "Or maybe you think it'll be the other way around?"

Jack said nothing.

"I don't know what in the hell is going on around here, but I'm walking out a free man."

Jack remained silent.

Sobrante narrowed his eyes.

"Why don't you say something?" Sobrante demanded.

"Got nothin' to say," Jack replied.

"Fine," Sobrante said as he walked across the room toward Jack. "Have it your way."

Sobrante was a big man, with two inches on Jack

and probably forty pounds. He was a man accustomed to getting his way and submitting others to his will. As a result, he did the same thing he always did. He lumbered forward and grabbed for Jack.

Jack let Sobrante get ahold of his shoulder and took a small step back. It was barely noticeable, but it was enough to cause the big man to lean into his toes instead of keeping his weight on his heels, and, as a result, throw himself off balance. Jack then pivoted to his left: again, just a very small move, but enough to expose the inside of Sobrante's knee.

Jack drove his heel into the man's knee, and the *pop* of Sobrante's ACL was sickening. The big man screamed and stumbled, further losing his balance. Jack made one more turn, put Sobrante into a head lock, and then turned again.

Snap!

Sobrante's eyes widened for a split second, and then he was dead.

Jack dropped the heavy body to the floor and turned back toward the door.

"I believe someone owes me a steak and a beer," he said.

.   .   .

Jack sat in the cold metal chair and looked around the office. It felt familiar, but something about it was different. It took a moment to grasp what had changed. He was still under a heavy dose of Thorazine, administered just after he received his steak, but *something* was indeed different.

Jack looked down at his hands and realized what it was. *No straitjacket.*

He looked over his shoulder and saw Grunewald, the orderly, standing in the corner. Then there came a creak from the corridor beyond the office, and he saw Doctor Barrister enter through another door and take up his position behind the desk.

The lights came on.

"How many lights, Jack?"

Jack did not respond.

"How did it make you feel?" Noah Barrister asked.

"How did *what* make me feel?"

"Killing that man. Mister..." Noah opened a folder and thumbed through the contents for a moment. "Sobrante."

"If you were telling the truth about him, I didn't feel much of anything."

"And what if we weren't?" Noah asked. "What if we tricked you?"

Jack did not respond.

"It doesn't matter," the doctor went on. "Because we weren't. He was exactly what Foster told you he was. You know, Jack—what you're doing here, what you're doing for us, isn't all that different from what you were doing with Delta."

Shit, Jack thought. *This son of a bitch knows who I am. Which means Grunewald knows, too. Does Foster know?*

"Are you surprised by that, Jack? That I know you were in Delta, I mean?"

"Doesn't matter," Jack replied.

"But you do understand that what you are doing here is important?"

"I was a volunteer in the Army. I never volunteered for this."

"But what if you could? What if you could become the hammer in the dark that America needs, executing the worst of the worst? The ones the law can't touch. Perhaps even those in power who think that they are above the law?"

"I'm not an assassin."

Doctor Noah Barrister laughed out loud.

"Come now, Mister Bonafide. Don't you think

that's splitting hairs just a little bit? You're trying to tell me that what you did in Central America and Vietnam wasn't wet work? You weren't an assassin then?"

"That was different!" Jack snapped.

"How many lights, Mister Bonafide!" Noah countered.

"*Two!*" Jack shouted. "I see two fucking lights, and ain't nothing you can say will make me think otherwise!"

Jack felt the jolt run through his back as Grunewald hit him with the cattle prod, and then everything went black.

Jack pulled in a sudden breath and looked around the room. The walls were grey, covered with a lack-luster coat of peeling paint. There was wire mesh on the windows, and a small amount of sunlight filtered in from an overcast sky.

In the corner, a television broadcast reruns of *The Andy Griffith Show*.

Jack was in the Day Room.

There were only a few other people there, but he recognized one of them: a man named Sid. Jack only knew this because Foster had mentioned him; told him that Sid was something of a project of Doctor Barrister's.

"Where are we?" Jack asked, directing the question toward Sid.

Sid turned to him.

"Somewhere else."

Jack let out a breath. Just asking the question had been challenging. He saw that Sid had a kit of some sort and a collection of paint and brushes, but he wasn't painting a picture. There was even an X-Acto knife on the table.

"What are you making?" Jack asked.

Sid looked back to Jack and smiled.

"A face."

"What do you mean?" Jack replied.

"I used to... make faces," Sid explained. "For Hollywood. Before I came here. Now I'm going to make faces for Doctor Barrister."

Sid took a moment to put some finishing touches to what he was working on, and then he held up the mask and put it to his face.

"Look, Jack," Sid said with obvious pride. "I'm you."

It was remarkable. The mask Sid had made looked exactly like Jack.

"That's really good, Sid," Jack said cautiously. "But why did you make that?"

"You okay?" a voice asked from behind Jack.

Jack looked over his shoulder and saw that it was Foster.

"Yeah," Jack said and then looked down at his straitjacket. "This thing hurts my arms."

"I'm trying to get you out of it," Foster said. "These things take time."

Jack looked to where Sid was sitting at one of the Formica-topped tables working on his faces.

"*He* doesn't have one," Jack said.

"Like I told you before," Foster said, "he's Doctor Barrister's prize pupil. Whatever the hell that means."

Sid smiled broadly and held up another project he was working on. It was a photo of Ronald Reagan with the Soviet Premier. Sid had drawn intricate designs around the two men.

"He'll be drawing flies soon," Sid said, and then returned to his faces.

Jack turned to Foster.

"He might need more medication."

The Home of David Kelvin

Washington D.C.
March 20, 1981

David Kelvin stood in his kitchen, cleaning his drinking glasses with a special cloth; a cloth that was made for tasks such as this and only those tasks. These cloths shared that attribute of specificity, as with many things in Kelvin's life.

He enjoyed the ritual of cleaning these glasses. A number of items in his home were broken on a regular basis by the cleaners—supposedly the best in all of Wesley Heights—and he wouldn't dare trust them with the safeguarding of his grandfather's crystal drinking glasses. Yes, they had almost certainly put the old man in the ground with a liver the size of a buffalo's, but they were family heirlooms all the same.

Another tool with a very specific task was his driver, Braxton, and one of those tasks had been to see that Jack Bonafide was committed to Saint Elizabeth's Mental Hospital. At first, it had seemed like a pretty simple solution. Braxton would have him interred there under a false identity, claiming that Bonafide was a dangerous schizophrenic, and the drugs Braxton would pump into the man's system before their arrival would seem to support that assessment.

Now, though, Kelvin was wondering if that had been the right move. Was it really necessary to put Bonafide on ice like that? Had the man really been a threat to him, or was he simply being vindictive? Was Tolya Rodin right? Had he acted out of spite?

This petulant need for reciprocity was one of Kelvin's less admirable traits, and he knew it. More often than not, it got him into trouble, and he was beginning to sense that this was one of those times.

He truly didn't give two shits about what happened to Jack Bonafide—or anyone else, for that matter—but he did care that this rash act seemed to have captured the attention of Richard Feldman, or Tolya Rodin, or *whoever* the hell he was. Kelvin had unknowingly performed a good deed for Tolya, and apparently the former Attorney General was now "in the club."

Of course, becoming the governor of New York would not be the worst of fates. It was just a matter of how deep he would allow himself to be pulled into this mess, and, of course, what price he would have to pay.

Upon considering this, Kelvin checked the clock

on the wall. The time had almost come to make the phone call. In the past hour alone, he had vacillated back and forth as to whether or not he was really going to do it, but he knew that he would. There was no turning back at this point. If he didn't make the call, the East Germans would not be pleased, and he would almost certainly be on the receiving end of some form of reprisal from the man in Leipzig.

The doorbell rang, and Kelvin turned to the hallway that lead to his front entrance. He looked around and sighed. Braxton was out on an errand and the housekeeper had the day off. It would seem that the task of answering the door had fallen to him. He carefully set the crystal glass down on the counter and surveyed his work. There was no hurry; even if he was no longer the Attorney General of the United States, he had no intention of jumping to attention for anyone.

He walked down the long hallway and approached the front door. He was just about to reach out and open it when he thought better of it. There was no reason to think he was in any danger, but, all the same, being cautious in dangerous times was never a bad thing.

Kelvin leaned forward and put his eye to the peep hole.

"What the hell?" he whispered.

Beyond the door was the Assistant Director of the CIA and some short kid with glasses. Kelvin knew that Michael Scarn had picked up the post after Mike Tresham had been elevated to the position of Director. It sure seemed like one hell of a fast ascent for both of them. Tresham's appointment had been especially surprising, considering what he had done at FBI Headquarters, but behind closed doors, it was rumored that the President thought the action would set a precedent that the new Director of the CIA was "not to be messed with," in the old man's words. He wasn't wrong about that, but Kelvin suspected that that train of thought had the potential to create problems with international relations further down the road.

Now, Tresham's newly minted right-hand man was at his door. Did he somehow know about his connection to Tolya Rodin? Well, there was no point in hemming and hawing about it, so Kelvin turned the knob and opened the door.

"Yes?" Kelvin asked, deciding to keep things all business.

"Mister Kelvin, I'm—" Scarn began, reaching into his pocket for his credentials.

"I know who you are," Kelvin said bluntly,

cutting Scarn off. "What can a lowly former Attorney General do for the Assistant Director of the CIA?"

"Well, sir, it's more a matter of your man Braxton. We'd like to have a word with him."

"He's out at the moment," Kelvin said.

Then Kelvin took a step back. It was almost imperceptible, but Scarn noticed it. Something about that question had literally set Kelvin back on his heels.

"Do you know when he'll be back?" Scarn pursued.

"No," Kelvin said, making it clear he would offer no further explanation.

"I'm sorry," Scarn said. "Have I done something to offend you?"

"Not at all," Kelvin said. "But I am thoroughly versed in what our various law enforcement agencies can and cannot do. I don't understand why the CIA is on my doorstep. Unless my home was moved to a foreign country while I was sleeping."

"Well, sir, it's just that no one can seem to track down papers for Rory Braxton. Meaning that he has no Green Card."

"I know what it means!" Kelvin snapped.

Scarn cocked his head to the side.

"So... what I'm suggesting is that you have an illegal with ties to a foreign intelligence agency in your employ. Doesn't that sound a little more like my jurisdiction?"

"Please!" Kelvin laughed. "I hardly consider MI6 to be an enemy agency."

"Call it what you want," Scarn said, "but I will talk to Braxton. Or we can bring in INS and see what else we find."

The mocking smile left Kelvin's face.

"Come back with a warrant."

Kelvin shut the door and scowled.

"*Shit.*"

He walked back into the kitchen and looked at the clock on the wall. Braxton would be back in a matter of minutes. Kelvin sure hoped like hell that the Brit would come in the back way like he always did, because shortly after, he would be on his way to the airport and out of the country.

Scarn closed the door of the sedan and stared out the windshield. *Jesus, Kelvin's one bitter son of a bitch,* he thought to himself. He also wondered if he had once been a lot more like Kelvin than he might care to admit, back before he began straightening himself out.

"He's dirty," Clark said. "You know he is."

"But I can't prove anything," Scarn countered. "That's the way this works. If I can't prove anything, I can't move on him."

"I can," Clark said, locking eyes with Scarn.

"You've been hanging out with Bonafide too much."

"Not lately," Clark shot back. "This is how we get him back, and you know it."

Clark had changed since Scarn first met him. He had hardened, and it was noticeable. Over the past few months alone, he had been in firefights and lost the only person who he probably considered a friend.

Scarn thought about it for a moment. Was he really going to do this? Was he really going to unleash an analyst with a grudge on the former Attorney General of the United States? He turned away from Clark to look at a figure walking across the street in front of them.

"Son of a bitch," Scarn said. "Is that who I think it is?"

Clark turned to look at the figure that had captured Scarn's attention.

"Yes, it is," he said. "It's Braxton."

The surly Englishman was crossing the street not twenty feet in front of their car, heading down the block around Kelvin's house.

"He's going in the back," Scarn surmised. "He has to be. Must be their SOP."

"Does that prove something?" Clark asked.

"Yes, it does. Even if I'm not sure what that is."

"That's the place," Mac Bonafide said, referencing the map in his hand before he stuffed it back in his pocket.

Carrie Davidson tapped the pistol secured to her hip and let out a breath. They had come a long way from Kulikovo, Siberia, to get there, but they had finally reached their destination.

The home of former US Attorney General David Kelvin.

"Fine," Carrie said. "Let's get it over with."

"Now hold on there, Hoss," Mac said. "What's the plan?"

Carrie stared at him for a moment.

"I can't take you seriously with those sunglasses on."

"You know the sun does a number on my eyes these days," Mac replied from behind the leopard print sunglasses he was wearing.

The pair he had been wearing since Siberia had broken during a mishap on the drive from the train station, and these had been the only pair he was able to scrounge.

"You look ridiculous," Carrie said.

"Look, is this a fucking assassination or a fashion show?"

"If it were a fashion show, you'd definitely win. You'd be the prettiest girl there."

"Fuck you."

"Pretty princess Mac Bonafide with her leopard print sunglasses."

"Fuck you twice," Mac said, but he couldn't help smiling.

"Look, the plan's simple." Carrie was suddenly back to the business at hand. "We go in the back, shoot this guy in the head, and then make a beeline for Saint Elizabeth's and break Jack out."

"Does he have it coming?" Mac asked.

"What do you mean?" Carrie replied.

"Well... we're going to kill this man. Does he

have it coming?"

"He was wrapped up in everything that happened last month. I can't say for sure what role he played, but his hands definitely aren't clean."

"Hmm."

"What?" Carrie asked indignantly.

"I don't know," Mac said. "Daniel told us what we'd be doing, so it's not like it's a surprise, but when you get down to brass tacks, when it's time to pull the trigger, it's different."

"We all die, Mac," Carrie said coldly. "It's just a matter of what the timeline looks like. Most folks are only waiting out the clock, so maybe we're just winding it a little faster."

Mac looked at her for a moment.

"I think you need to talk to someone. Like a professional."

Carrie ignored the comment and walked toward the house.

Kelvin turned to the sound of the rear door opening as Rory Braxton entered. Braxton stopped in the hallway. Right away, he could see that something was wrong.

"What is it?" Braxton asked.

"The Assistant *fucking* Director of the *fucking* CIA was just here," Kelvin snarled. "And I can't help but think it has something to do with a certain operative of theirs going missing."

"No one can connect you to that," Braxton said quickly.

"The knock on *my* door seems to suggest otherwise," Kelvin countered.

"So, what do we do about it?"

"We get you out of the country," Kelvin said, and then he held up a hand in a placating gesture. "Not forever; just until this blows over. And it will."

"How can you be so sure?"

"The Governor of New York doesn't have to answer as many questions as an out-of-work former Attorney General."

Braxton nodded his understanding.

"And you're certain this Russian will honor his word?"

"I have no reason to think he won't," Kelvin said. "And he stands to lose just as much as I do if I go running my mouth. No, I think we're all in this boat together."

"Where will I go?" Braxton asked.

"I already have a standing extraction plan for you. Myself, as well, if needed. You'll go to an undisclosed location in Ontario and lay low for a few months. Then we'll decide if it's safe for you to return, or if we need to move you again."

Carrie had watched the man go in the rear door, but she wasn't sure who he was. She knew that Kelvin had some kind of guard detail, but she hadn't put much thought into it. With Mac on her side, she doubted they would run into anything they couldn't handle.

"He didn't lock it," Mac said as they approached the door.

"How can you be sure?" Carrie asked.

"Middle of the day. Nice neighborhood. People are stupid. Pick your poison," Mac said. "But it ain't locked."

Carrie reached out and turned the doorknob. He was right: it wasn't locked. She drew her Beretta M1951 and gestured to Mac that they were going in.

"Please take those off," Carrie said, indicating the sunglasses. "You look ridiculous."

"I really don't like you right now," Mac replied, but he removed the sunglasses nonetheless.

Carrie discreetly opened the door and stepped into the hallway, Mac close behind her. She could hear two men talking. She held up her hand to motion for Mac to stop.

She turned back to him.

He nodded.

Carrie rounded the corner and found the two men standing in a large living area. She recognized Kelvin right away, but not the other man. She suspected he was Kelvin's driver, judging by how he was dressed.

"Don't move!" Carrie ordered.

Braxton ignored the command. He turned and started to reach for something.

Carrie pushed her gun forward aggressively and snarled at him.

"Don't!"

Braxton froze. He saw something in her eyes; something vicious.

"That's what I thought," she said. "Two fingers, out of your jacket."

She had already identified the bulge of a shoulder holster on Braxton's left side. The Brit reached for the Ruger pistol and removed it with two fingers. He dropped it to the floor and took a step back. He noticed that Kelvin gave him a disapproving look, but what the hell was he supposed to do? This woman was clearly no amateur.

Mac circled the room and took up a position behind Kelvin.

"What is this?" Kelvin demanded. "Do you know who I am?"

"Who you are," Carrie said, "is why we are here. Now get on your knees."

"What do you intend to do?" Kelvin asked.

"This doesn't have to be difficult," Carrie said. "Unless you make it so."

"A fighting chance," Braxton blurted.

"What?" Carrie asked, confused.

Braxton turned to where Mac was standing.

"You're a strapping fellow," Braxton said. "I just want a fighting chance. I don't want to be shot in the back of the head like some fucking amateur. I want to go down swinging."

Mac looked to Carrie, who was screwing a suppressor onto her pistol.

"This is stupid," Carrie said. "But seeing as you've only got a year to live, I might as well let you have your fun."

It was a calculated risk on Braxton's part. This man looked like a monster, but he knew there was no way he could take both him and the woman while they were both armed. If he could get through this man, however, he had a chance of taking the woman down.

Mac Bonafide reached out and set his pistol down on the fireplace mantle. He cracked his knuckles and stepped forward.

Braxton bared his fists, and his upper lip curled back.

Then pink mist, and he collapsed to the floor.

"*Jesus Christ!*" Kelvin gasped.

Carrie lowered her pistol.

"What the hell, Carrie?" Mac pleaded.

"You didn't actually think I was going to let that happen, did you?" Carrie asked.

Mac walked back to the fireplace and retrieved his pistol.

"It would have been a nice change of pace."

Kelvin looked down at Braxton's body and had the sudden realization that he might soon be joining him.

Carrie turned to Kelvin and raised her pistol again.

"Wait!" Kelvin nearly shouted. "I have something you want!"

"Unless you're a fan of high waisted jeans," Carrie said, "I really doubt you do."

"You're from the CIA! You have to be!" Kelvin

pressed on.

"We're not."

"I have information about a Soviet agent!"

"I don't care," Carrie said, and she pulled back the hammer on her pistol.

"He had one of your agents detained in Saint Elizabeth's Mental Hospital!"

Carrie stopped.

"What did you say?" she asked.

Kelvin let out a breath; his lie was working. But would it be enough to extricate him from this mess?

"What do we do?" Clark asked.

Scarn turned to the analyst.

"I like my job," Scarn said. "And I'm not sure following up on this is the best way to keep it."

"Jack would do it for you," Clark said pointedly. "You know he would. Without a second thought."

Scarn drummed his fingers on the steering wheel.

"Shit."

Scarn and Clark had opted to circle around to the back of the house, to cover the same way they saw

Braxton going in. Scarn stopped at the rear door and drew his weapon. The door was open. He turned to Clark and waited.

"What?" Clark asked.

"Don't you have a firearm?"

"Why in the hell would I have a gun? I'm an analyst on leave."

"Jesus," Scarn groaned. He reached down to his ankle, drew a small .38 revolver that was holstered there, and handed it to Clark.

"This is illegal," Clark said as he took the pistol. "Just so you know."

"You really do have a personality disorder," Scarn said, pushing the door open with his foot.

"Pot, this is kettle," Clark said. "You're black."

"His name is Jack Bonafide. This... this Soviet agent thought Bonafide was in the way, so he had him committed. Pretended he was a schizophrenic." Kelvin paused and looked down at Braxton's body. He couldn't believe this was happening. Who in the hell were these people? "He's there right now."

"We know he is," Carrie said. "We just didn't know why. Which leads to the question: how do you know all this?"

"They blackmailed me."

"Folks usually have to have something to hide to get blackmailed," Mac interjected.

"Look, it doesn't matter what I did!" Kelvin shot back.

"That's a matter of opinion," Mac replied.

"Do you want Bonafide out of there or not?"

"We know where he is," Carrie said. "What do we need *you* for?"

"Doctor Barrister," Kelvin said. "I know him. I can help you. He runs the hospital."

Mac looked at Carrie and nodded.

"Don't move!" a voice shouted. "Down on the ground! Now!"

"I don't think so," Carrie said.

She turned and pointed her pistol at Assistant Director of the CIA Michael Scarn. Then she realized who he was.

"What in the hell are you doing here?" Scarn asked.

"Carrie?" Clark followed up.

"Family reunion," Mac said with a smile as he picked up his weapon.

This caught Scarn's attention.

"Mac? What in the hell?"

CHAPTER 2

Saint Elizabeth's Mental Hospital
The Office of Doctor Noah Barrister
March 20, 1981

JACK STOOD in his room and stared at the wall. There were chalk markings all over it. They were like scenes out of an apocalypse. He looked down and saw the stick of chalk in his hand. Was this *his* apocalypse? Was this his own dark future he was seeing on the wall before him? Had he drawn this?

Then he had another realization: he wasn't wearing the straitjacket anymore. He stretched his arms out. It felt good. His body felt good, but his brain was fractured. It was getting harder to hold onto memories. Not only memories, but also what was happening in the present. Perhaps this dark future on the wall was the only thing he could really hold onto. Was it the future, though? Or was it a memory?

He dropped the chalk and looked around the room. There was nothing. A bed, a toilet, and a sink. It was dark. Was it day or night? There was no way to know. At this point, he had lost track of how long he had been in this place.

"You gonna cry?" a gravelly voice called out from the corner of the room. "Looks like you're gonna cry."

Jack didn't reply. He knew what this was and who the voice belonged to. It hadn't happened to him before, but Mac had told him about it. It figured that, after Mac was gone, their Uncle John would eventually come for him.

"I didn't think my brother raised no pussies," Uncle John said. "Guess I was wrong."

Jack opened his mouth to respond and then stopped himself. Starting to respond to the voices in his head was probably not a good idea.

"Answer me, boy," Uncle John said.

Jack declined.

"Did you draw that?"

This was a different voice, but a familiar one. It was Foster.

"Did I?" Jack asked as he looked at the horrific scene scrawled across the cement wall in chalk.

Foster entered the room and looked back to the open door.

"What is it?" Foster asked.

Jack thought for a moment and remembered that he had drawn it.

"A plane," Jack said. "A plane burning in the desert."

"Was that something you saw?" Foster asked.

"Maybe. At first, I thought it was the future, but maybe it's the past."

"How do you feel, Jack?" Foster asked.

"I don't know," Jack replied. "I don't know anything anymore." He turned to Foster. "Who am I? Who *was* I?"

"Who do you think you were?" Foster asked, probing.

"I think I... I think I was in the Army?"

"You were," Foster said, looking back to the door again. He suspected that Doctor Barrister knew more about Jack than he was letting on, but he didn't know what that was. "Do you remember anything else?"

Jack turned to look at Foster.

"I kill people."

"You do, Jack," Foster said. He took a step toward the former Delta operator. "And you're good at it. But I'm your friend, right?"

"Yes," Jack said. "I think you are, Foster."

"Just remember that, if the time comes that it matters."

He had passed out again. Perhaps it was another dose of the the Thorazine that had knocked him out. Jack focused his vision and saw that he was back in the Day Room.

"We all go black," a voice beside him said. "Eventually."

Jack turned and saw Sid sitting in a wheelchair.

"Your legs work?" Jack asked.

"Legs work fine," Sid said. "Wheelchairs are just more comfortable than the hard plastic ones."

Something about the man had changed. He seemed more lucid. He was wearing a t-shirt with the sleeves cut off, and Jack recognized the tattoo on his arm.

"Ranger?" Jack asked.

Sid looked down at the Ranger tab tattooed on his left arm as if he had forgotten it was there.

"Sixty-eight," Sid replied. "You?"

"I think so," Jack said. "It's hard to remember. Thoughts keep... slipping away."

"It's the Thorazine," Sid said, smiling. "Enjoy it while you can."

Jack looked down at what Sid was working on with his hands and saw that it was another photo of President Reagan meeting with Brezhnev.

Sid saw Jack observing him, and his smile broadened.

"He'll be drawing flies soon."

Saint Elizabeth's Mental Hospital
The Office of Doctor Noah Barrister
March 20, 1981

"Okay, you fucking redneck," Doctor Barrister said sharply. "How many lights do you see?"

Jack looked around the office, then to his hands, and then to Noah Barrister, sitting across from him on the opposite side of the big desk.

Jack wasn't restrained in any way. He looked over his shoulder and didn't see the big German standing behind him with the cattle prod.

There was no one to stop him from killing this man. So, why hadn't he tried?

Jack looked up at the light array. There were two.

"Two lights," Jack said. "I see two lights."

Doctor Barrister let out a deep sigh.

"This is the problem, Jack. This is just another sign of how deeply troubled you are, and of how fractured your mind is. You claim to see only two lights when, clearly, there are three."

"There are *two*," Jack insisted.

Doctor Barrister clicked a ballpoint pen repeatedly. He glared at Jack over the rims of his glasses.

"Do you deny that you see things that aren't there?" Doctor Barrister said. "Do you deny that you hear a ringing in your ears? That your hands tremor?"

Jack looked down at his hands. They were trembling. He thought about the questions for a moment and realized that he *could* hear a faint ringing in his ears. He tried to remember how long these things had been going on, but, as usual, trying to nail down his memories was like struggling to catch a fish while swimming in an ocean of quicksilver.

Was this man right? Was the doctor trying to help him?

Jack looked up at the light array. It really did look like there were two lights. Was he wrong? It did seem like one of them wanted to split off into another light. Were there really three?

"No, you fucking Mary," the gravely voice called out from the corner. "There are two goddamn lights, and if you don't give this squirrely son of a bitch a Texarkana smile, I'll do it for you."

Jack turned toward the voice before focusing back on Doctor Barrister.

"What do you see there?" Doctor Barrister asked, inclining his head toward the corner of the room.

Jack shook his head.

"How many lights, Jack? *How many* do you see?"

Jack's posture slumped. He was tired.

He looked back up at the light array and shook his head.

"I see two lights."

'Have it your way," Doctor Barrister said. He leaned back in his chair and checked his watch. "It's about time, anyway."

.   .   .

"They've given you some freedom," Foster said as he helped Jack down the hallway. "If you want my advice, don't do anything stupid. You know? They're testing you, you know?"

Jack stopped and turned to Foster.

"I have a home," Jack said. "I come from somewhere. Even if I can't quite remember where it is."

Foster's eyes softened.

"I know, Jack, but I also don't know where that is." He looked down the hallway to Doctor Barrister's office and then back to Jack. "*They* know. Barrister, for sure, and probably Grunewald, too. I'm not that deep in the loop."

"If I could just get these *fucking*... drugs out of my system for a little bit—"

"No!" Foster cut him off. "Don't start down that road or you'll force my hand. I like you, Jack, but I also like my job. I think what we're doing here is important."

"More important... than my freedom?" Jack asked.

"The needs of the many, Jack, outweigh the needs of the few. I may not know your full history, but I can tell you were military. You know what I'm saying is true." Foster reached into his pocket and retrieved one of the syringes that Jack knew were full of either Thorazine or adrenaline. "Don't force my hand, Jack. Just go along to get along and everything will be fine. You'll get more freedom, and things will be good. I promise."

The Home of David Kelvin
Washington D.C.
March 20, 1981

"What are you two doing here?" Scarn asked. "And what in the hell happened to Braxton?"

"Carrie shot him," Mac said.

"Why?" Scarn demanded. Then he noticed Carrie had not lowered her weapon. "What in the hell is going on here?"

"Scarn, Clark," Carrie said, "weapons on the floor, please."

Clark complied.

"What are you doing?" Scarn asked Clark.

"She said 'please,'" Clark explained.

"Now you, Scarn," Carrie said.

"Or what?" Scarn asked. "You'll shoot me?"

"It's not my first choice," Carrie said. "But bad things happen to good people all the time."

"I need help!" Kelvin demanded, turning his attention to Scarn.

"Shut up!" Scarn and Carrie said simultaneously.

Seizing the opportunity created by Kelvin's pleading, Mac snatched Scarn's pistol out of the Assistant Director's hand.

Scarn took a step back.

"Sorry, Scarn," Mac said. "It's the best way to defuse this situation. I'll give it back when this is over."

"What are you two doing here?" Scarn asked again.

"Mister Kelvin here has a date with destiny," Mac said. "What are you doing here?"

"We came to question *him*," Scarn said, indicating Braxton's corpse.

"Well, looks like that horse has bolted," Mac quipped.

Clark took a knee and began going through Braxton's pockets.

"Why were you looking for him?" Carrie asked.

"We think he might know where Jack is," Clark replied.

Mac and Carrie exchanged a glance, which Scarn picked up on.

"What do you know?" he asked.

"Jack's in Saint Elizabeth's," Carrie said.

Clark looked up.

"The mental hospital?" he asked.

"That's right," Mac said. "We just have to bump off Cary Grant here, and then we'll go bail Jack out."

"You think I look like Cary Grant?" Kelvin asked, obviously flattered.

"I think you missed the part where he just said they're going to kill you," Clark interjected.

"There has to have been some misunderstanding here. I still don't understand what I did that warrants my death!" Kelvin demanded.

"Let's rewind," Carrie said, lowering her weapon and turning to Kelvin. "To the part where you were talking about a Soviet agent and Doctor Barrister."

Saint Elizabeth's Mental Hospital
Washington D.C
March 20, 1981

Standing in the dark tunnel beneath the hospital, Doctor Barrister fidgeted with the old lighter and again attempted to light his cigarette. Once again, just as it had three times before, a breeze drifting through the tunnel snuffed out his light. He sighed.

Doctor Barrister heard a sharp, scraping sound, and a hand holding a lit match emerged from the darkness of the sub-basement tunnel, offering to light his Marlboro Red.

"*Jesus!*" Doctor Barrister gasped.

"I am as far from Jesus as you can get," Arkady said as he lit the cigarette and then blew out the match.

Doctor Barrister inhaled deeply from his cigarette and then said, "I hope you understand that these little meetings make things much more difficult for me."

"I care not for how difficult your life is," Arkady said bluntly. "If you wanted a simple life, perhaps you should have chosen a different path."

Doctor Barrister wanted to push back, but he had learned during the course of their last interaction that Arkady Radovich had no flex. He was as constant and unwavering as a piece of stone.

"What is it you want?" Doctor Barrister asked pointedly.

"When will he be ready?" Arkady asked.

Doctor Barrister shook his head.

"What you want... what you are asking for is impossible."

"In the Soviet Union, we did it all the time," Arkady insisted. "It was practically the national pastime."

"But the timeline," Doctor Barrister said. "It's just too short. If I had another six months, maybe, but even then, it's questionable at best. The training he went through has hardened his mind. I know because I helped to design it. I can't crack a shell like that in the timeframe you've given me. I didn't even know who he was when I first suggested I could turn him!"

"More drugs?" Arkady asked.

"Don't you think I've thought of that? Christ, his heart should have stopped by now with all the shit we've been pumping into him. Hell, it should have *exploded* out of his chest."

"You have been given your mandate," Arkady said pointedly.

Doctor Barrister looked around for a moment and then turned his eyes back to Arkady.

"Look, at least consider this other man I've been working on. He's fully prepped and ready to go! He was only supposed to be the test run to make sure my techniques worked, but I honestly think he could be your trigger man."

Arkady seemed to consider this for a moment and then nodded.

"Tell me more."

"Don't we have some business to conduct first?" Doctor Barrister asked, obviously uncomfortable.

Arkady let out a sigh and reached into his jacket. He handed Doctor Barrister a thick envelope. Barrister grabbed it, but Arkady held fast and smiled.

"Is this what you envisioned for yourself?" Arkady asked. "When you started down this path?"

"I never signed up for this Coal Chamber bullshit," Barrister snarled, yanking the envelope away. "We were doing good work with the MK Ultra program. *Important* work! Then they pulled the fucking rug out from under us and tried to make us look like the villains."

"Did it ever occur to you that perhaps you *are* the villain?" Arkady quipped.

"At this point," Doctor Barrister replied, "I don't really give a shit. As long as I'm a rich villain."

French Street
Buenos Aires, Argentina

March 20, 1981

Daniel Flynn sat on the small cot in the equally small room she had rented in the boarding house on French Street. She appreciated Buenos Aires in a way that not many would, considering how she had spent her formative years there killing Nazis.

That had been the original mandate of the Coal Chamber: to vanish from existence those that were deserving but the law could not touch. In the very beginning, it had been just her; then, over time, other recruits were brought on board. If she was being honest about it—honest with *herself*—she wasn't sure which version was better.

A part of her that she didn't like to acknowledge appreciated the simplicity of being the lone assassin with an M-14 or a suppressed .22 caliber pistol. She would receive her assignments from her mole at Interpol and do the job. It was a mechanical existence. Then, when the job was over, she would drink for as long as it took to burn away the demons before crying herself to sleep.

Then she would wake and repeat the process. Purge, kill, repeat.

After enough time had passed and enough damage had been done, the cancer came. After that came the butchers with their surgeries, and she was left with less than she had been.

This did nothing to diminish her anger.

Purge, kill, repeat.

The team had grown. The supposed "ex-agents" were sent to her to augment her forces.

"*I don't want a team.*"

She remembered speaking those words to the Assistant Director of the CIA ten years prior.

"*No one cares what you want,*" he had replied. "*Just do your job. Get the Coal Chamber project up and running. You're the only one who can.*"

And so, she did. She found them and trained them as best she could. Then she would check into a motel.

Purge, kill, repeat.

Daniel stood up from the cot and walked to the single table in her room. Her duffel bag sat upon it, and she unzipped it. From within, she retrieved the photo album.

Goldmann Family

. . .

The words were emblazoned across the cover in gold leaf. It was her family photo album; all that remained of them. Daniel thought back to that summer as an exchange student, living with the Goldmann family in Denmark. The war had seemed so far away.

Then, suddenly, it was on her doorstep.

A quiet beeping broke the silence of her reverie. She turned her gaze back to the duffel bag on the table. It was the secure phone. Daniel returned to the photo album and ran her hand across the leather cover. Her memories were a contrast of days spent in sunlit fields and nights spent hunting high ranking German officers with her Krag Jorgenson rifle.

Before then, she had never even held a weapon, much less tried to take a headshot at three hundred meters. It was on-the-job training, and when she had first set about exacting her pound of flesh from the German Army following the murder of the Goldmann family, the survival rate of her targets had been high. She missed the Germans more often than she hit them, but that soon changed.

It did not take long for her kill rate to hit one hundred percent. She had a talent for it.

The beeping again.

Daniel turned back to the duffel bag and grimaced.

"Fine," she hissed.

She stood up and crossed the room, then fished the phone out of the bag, and hit the button to receive the call.

She said nothing.

"Is this Daniel Flynn?" a voice asked from the other end of the line.

"Who's asking?" Daniel replied.

"The Director of the CIA," Mike Tresham replied curtly. His annoyance was evident.

"Director, no less," Daniel said indifferently.

"You don't sound very impressed," Tresham replied. He wasn't seeking compliments, but rather attempting to suss out the psychological profile of the person he was talking to.

"I think I've had my socks on longer than the last guy was Director," Daniel replied. "But I'm bowing to the throne in spirit if not body."

Tresham couldn't help but smile. She had a mouth on her, but he liked people who spoke their mind.

"I need a SITREP," Tresham said.

Daniel raised an eyebrow.

"A SITREP?" she asked.

"Yes," Tresham replied. "You do know how to give one, right?"

"It's just that it would be a SITREP for the past thirteen years."

"Where are you now?" Tresham asked.

Daniel looked around.

"A room."

"A room where?" Tresham pushed.

"Buenos Aires."

"What active protocols are you running?"

"Only one," Daniel replied. "But you won't like it."

"Enlighten me," Tresham pushed.

"We're assassinating David Kelvin."

There was a noticeable pause on the line.

"May I ask why?" Tresham pursued.

"He has skeletons in his closet," Daniel said. "The type that demand retribution."

The only reason Tresham had not immediately exploded upon finding out one of his own operatives was preparing to kill the former Attorney General of the United States was because he suspected Kelvin was all kinds of dirty. In fact, he thought that there was compelling evidence to suggest that the man was somehow wrapped up in the attack on CIA Headquarters, even if he couldn't prove anything.

"Look, I'm no fan of Mister Kelvin, but if you're trying to tell me we're going to be responsible for killing—" Tresham glanced down at the phone on his desk to confirm it was a black line, the most secure possible connection—"a former US Attorney General, I need a *damn* good reason."

"Nazi gold," Daniel said curtly.

"What?"

"Go back through his financials. Check his pedigree. His family didn't have money. At least, not much. So, where did his wealth come from? Might have something to do with him being in Germany after the war as a public relations officer."

"You're trying to tell me that David Kelvin financed his political career with Nazi gold?"

"Yes."

"And, in your book, that's enough reason to kill him?"

"In my book, yes, it is," Daniel replied. "But that's not the whole story."

"Go on."

"The whole story, Mister Director, is who paid him with that Nazi gold, and what he did for it."

"I have a feeling I'm not going to like this," Tresham said. "But before we get into that, I need to put the brakes on this operation. At least until I have the facts sorted out."

"That is your prerogative."

"Who's running point?"

"Carrie Davidson."

"You're shitting me."

"I shit you not," Daniel said.

She opened her mouth to tell Tresham about the phone call David Kelvin would be making in under twenty-four hours, but she stopped herself. Daniel knew how these things worked. The more people she let into the circle, the noisier it would become, and then the odds of mission success would drop sharply.

No, she would keep this new Director occupied for the time being. She had no intention of reeling in Carrie Davidson or stopping the operation. Even at the request of the Director of the CIA.

The Home of David Kelvin
Washington D.C.
March 20, 1981

Carrie, Scarn, Mac, Clark, and Kelvin walked across the front lawn to where Scarn had parked his sedan. He turned back to Carrie.

"So, what happens now?" Scarn asked.

"You can't kill me," Kelvin interjected. "I know more."

Carrie turned to Kelvin.

"You're not offering much in the way of an alternative. Unless you want to start tell us about this Soviet agent?"

Kelvin smirked.

Carrie stared at him.

"Well?" she asked.

"Sorry, sweetheart. You'll have to work a little harder than that to get into my pants," Kelvin sneered.

Carrie stepped forward and slammed her knee into Kelvin's groin. The man dropped to the sidewalk with a howl as Carrie put her sunglasses back on.

"Was *that* what you meant?" Carrie asked. "Talk to me like a street whore again and you'll be looking for your balls in the gutter."

"You're way scarier than the last time I saw you," Clark said, shaking his head.

A faint beeping emitted from the car, and Scarn reached into the back seat to retrieve the large cellular phone.

"This is Scarn."

"Scarn, this is Tresham. Where are you?"

"Just running some errands," Scarn lied. "Busy work."

"You haven't heard anything from Carrie Davidson, have you?" Tresham asked.

Scarn turned to Carrie.

"Carrie Davidson?" he asked, briefly making eye contact with her.

"Scarn, why are you repeating my question?" Tresham asked.

"Just surprised, is all. I thought Davidson was in the wind."

"She was, but I now have reason to believe she's running point on a CIA operation."

"How is that possible?"

"It's a long story. I'll debrief you when you get back," Tresham said. "But full disclosure, you'll wish you'd been left out of the loop on this one. When are you back onsite?"

"Should be by close of business."

"Come straight to my office."

"Roger that," Scarn replied, and he hit the button to end the call.

"Do you think he knows?" Carrie asked.

"Doubtful, but I think he knows I'm not being completely forthcoming with him. It's probably best if I head back." Scarn looked down at Kelvin. "What about him?"

"He's coming with us," Carrie said.

"And where, pray tell, is that?" Scarn asked.

"We're getting Jack out of the nuthouse," Carrie replied. "And then Rhett Butler here is going to spill the beans about this supposed Soviet agent."

Saint Elizabeth's Mental Hospital
March 20, 1981

"What does that guy have against the President?" Jack asked.

Foster finished his daily check of Jack's room and then turned to him.

"Doctor Barrister is trying to help Sid with that," Foster said. "He's trying to help all of you."

"Are you sure about that?" Jack followed up.

"About what?"

"That he's trying to help?"

Jack had noticed over the past day that he was beginning to feel more lucid. It seemed that his thoughts were easier to hold onto; words were becoming easier to string together. He wasn't sure if it was an effect of some change to his medication or if he was actually starting to build up a resistance to the dosage.

"What else would he be trying to do?" Foster asked in an accusatory tone.

"It just doesn't make sense," Jack pursued. "If you guys are trying to help, trying to make things better, why am I a prisoner?"

"You don't remember what you were like when you came to us, Jack," Foster shot back. "You were a mess. You needed us. You needed Doctor Barrister."

"And now?"

Foster seemed momentarily lost for words.

"I'm not having this conversation with you," Foster said, looking at his watch. "I'll be back in fifteen to take you down the hall."

Foster only ever took Jack two places: either for "treatment" or "down the hall." The former meant time with Doctor Barrister, and the latter meant a fight.

"I don't want to do that anymore," Jack said.

"Well, it's not up to you."

"So I am," Jack said decisively.

"What?"

"A prisoner."

"If that's what you want to call it, Jack. It needs to be done, and you're the one to do it."

"And if I refuse?" Jack asked.

Foster let out a sigh.

"I like you, Jack. You know that. I don't want to see anything bad happen to you, and I think we both know what that looks like."

Jack closed his hands. He could feel that they were stronger. Something was happening. The drugs in his system no longer felt as strong as they once had. He just needed to buy some more time.

"Fine."

Despite the feeling of energy starting to surge through his system, Jack felt like this walk was taking much longer than normal. He also noticed that there were fewer orderlies this time. He only counted two in addition to Foster. Grunewald was nowhere to be seen. That was good, because Jack figured the big German was the only one who might give him a run for his money.

"This is another bad guy, Jack," Foster said as they lead him down the long hallway to the padded room that had become their gladiator coliseum. "Not sure if you know about that attack on CIA Headquarters last month? This guy was one of them. One of the guys that staged the attack."

Jack stopped dead in his tracks and turned to Foster.

"What?"

"Guess you didn't hear about it," Foster said. "Yeah, these guys hit Langley hard. Rockets and everything. It was crazy. Government tried to keep it out of the press as best they could. They held onto this guy for a month trying to get him to talk, but no go. Now they just need him to go away without a messy trial. That's where we come in. Specifically, that's where *you* come in."

It can't be, Jack thought to himself. He did remember the attack and his involvement, even if those memories were a bit of a blur. There was only one person it could be.

The guy from the hallway. The one he'd saved with the tourniquet after killing his buddies. In a weird way, it made sense. If this place was some sort of black operations clearing house for the worst of the worst, Yahontov would definitely fit the bill.

"Guess it slipped below my radar," Jack said, turning back to the hallway.

· · ·

"I don't see why I have to be here," Kelvin said from the back seat of the sedan.

Carrie looked at him in the rearview mirror.

"The alternative was shooting you and leaving you on your lawn," she replied. "Should I turn the car around and go down that route?"

"I don't like it here," Kelvin said.

Carrie picked up on something in the tone of his voice: something more than just being unhappy with the current situation. She stared at him for a moment.

"You've been here before, haven't you?" Carrie asked.

"I don't want to talk about it!" Kelvin snapped.

There it was again. A shift. Almost as if his entire personality had changed for just a moment. Even something about his face had seemed to change.

"This place is a fucking rabbit hole," Mac said. "Literally and metaphorically."

"Do you know your way around?" Carrie asked.

"I wouldn't say that. I came out a side access door into this parking lot." Mac stared for a moment at the Mental Hospital. "We'll go back in the same way. Stick together, put down anyone who gets in our way."

"Doesn't that seem a little extreme?" Clark asked.

"I'm not saying we have to kill them," Mac replied. "Just put them out of action. Jack's my brother. I'm going to do whatever it takes to get him out."

"I've been looking for him for the past month," Clark shot back. "I was the only one."

Mac held up his hands in an *"I surrender"* gesture.

"Okay, okay," Mac said. "I get it. We've all got skin in the game here."

"I'm *not* going in there with you!" Kelvin interjected.

"You're right about that," Carrie said.

She turned around, jabbed Kelvin in the side of the neck with a hypodermic needle, and worked the plunger. He winced for a moment, and then he was out.

"Holy shit!" Clark yelled. "Is he dead?"

"Unfortunately, no," Carrie replied. "But he'll be out for a few hours. Long enough for us to do what needs to be done without him getting in the way."

The Office of the Director

CIA Headquarters
Langley, Virginia
March 20, 1981

Director of the CIA Mike Tresham dropped the phone back into the cradle and turned to the woman who—at least up until her recently announced impending retirement—was his secretary.

"Well, *this* is a fucking mess," Tresham groused.

"I told you," Eleanor replied. "Pandora."

Tresham turned back to the stack of sealed envelopes on his desk.

"Did that last experience teach you nothing?" Eleanor inquired.

"I can't just pretend they're not there!" Tresham declared. He reached out to the pile and retrieved the next one.

"Homicide detectives," Eleanor said.

"What?" Tresham asked.

"They're like homicide detectives, those folders. They never have good news."

"I didn't know you were funny," Tresham dead-panned as he ripped open the next folder and pulled out the contents. "Operation Overwatch. Even the name sounds bad."

Eleanor took a few steps backward.

Tresham noticed.

"Let me guess, you know about this one, too?"

"Not from personal experience, but I've heard the name. The outfit operating out of Saint Elizabeth's Mental Hospital?"

Tresham continued thumbing through the papers and then stopped.

"Holy shit! Are we *executing* people in the fucking nuthouse?"

"Just the worst of the worst," Eleanor said, in what Tresham took to be her attempt at a reassuring tone. "The ones that need to disappear for the good of the many."

"Like who?"

"I'm not privy, but they are all people that the Agency needs disposing of without a lot of fuss." Eleanor paused. "At least, that's my understanding. As I said, I'm not privy."

"Well, this shit stops now!"

Tresham reached for his phone.

"I wouldn't do that." Eleanor stopped him.

"Why not?"

"They'll burn it to the ground. Erase it. It will be

as if it never happened. They're good at it; it's what they do. You remember what I said about MK Ultra?"

"Yes."

"They're using those same techniques in Saint Elizabeth's. In the beginning, they were trying to turn enemy agents. That was the mandate."

"And now?"

"When they couldn't turn them, they were told to make them disappear. It didn't take long for it to become a clearing house; a sort of roach motel for the unwanted," Eleanor said. "They check in, but... well, you know."

"We just kill them."

"After a fashion."

Tresham relaxed his posture.

"So, if you were me," he said, "what would you do?"

"The last time I checked the personnel files, Doctor Barrister was still running our division at the hospital."

"You knew about this?" Tresham asked.

"Not all of it, and besides, it's none of my business," Eleanor pushed back.

"Understood," Tresham acquiesced. "I just need your help."

"Give it a day," Eleanor said. "Think over how you want to handle this, then invite Barrister to lunch. If you want him to shut down the program without too much fuss, you'll need to give him someplace to go."

"Early retirement?" Tresham asked.

Eleanor shook her head.

"Not for him. He won't have it. You'll have to come up with something else. A job."

"A *job*?" Tresham asked in disbelief. "This guy is operating a slaughterhouse in direct violation of the constitution of the United States, and you want me to offer him a job?"

"Oh, I'm sorry," Eleanor said. "I didn't realize that we were running the Langley chapter of the Boy Scouts of America."

Tresham glared at her for a moment and then shook his head.

"No, I'm not bargaining with this guy. We're going old school on this. Wrath of God style."

"That's your decision to make," Eleanor said.

"Get the Bravo assault team leader on the line. We're hitting this place today."

Saint Elizabeth's Mental Hospital

The Office of Doctor Noah Barrister
March 20, 1981

Doctor Noah Barrister knelt beside the old safe and carefully stacked the neatly wrapped packages of hundred-dollar bills into the steel briefcase. He had been offered the use of a numbered Swiss bank account, and even though he believed the reassurances that it would be very secure, he did not like the idea of someone else having control over his money.

He smiled at that. *His* money. It was all his.

This briefcase alone contained upward of one hundred thousand dollars. There was nearly a million in the floor safe in his home. It had taken years of double dipping and dirty dealings to get this far, and he had no intention of letting it all slip through his fingers now. Even if it did seem like the end was near.

Agreeing to work with Tolya Rodin was the final straw. Noah understood that, by doing so, he was crossing a threshold into a dark realm; one from which he could not return.

Not that he cared much. After all, what in the hell had the CIA—or the United States, for that matter—ever done for him? He knew exactly what they had done. They had destroyed his life's work by shutting down MK Ultra and then making him the scapegoat for everything that was supposedly wrong with the program.

What had he earned for all his hard work? He had been relegated to running a wet works shop masquerading as an insane asylum.

The problem was that Noah Barrister had always believed in America and in what he was doing. He believed that his role developing MK Ultra for the CIA had been important. Even when his name had been smeared and he was shipped off to Saint Elizabeth's, he took the new posting very seriously. He had developed a team of "orderlies" comprised of former field officers—mostly disgraced—and other spooks of unknown origin.

Under his watch, they had disposed of scores of men designated as enemies of the state who were beyond rehabilitation. Effectively, these people needed to be "thrown away," and Doctor Noah Barrister had become America's garbage man.

Then, agents operating on behalf of other interests had come calling. Apparently, the idea had gotten out that Noah might be amenable to getting rid of some "bonus" garbage. For a tidy fee, of course.

That was how Jack Bonafide had showed up on his doorstep. Rory Braxton, operating on behalf of the former US Attorney General, needed that redneck Jack Bonafide to go away.

Jack would disappear, just like all the others had, but Noah had figured he could get some mileage out of him first. Make things interesting.

Then Arkady Radovich had paid him a visit one evening on behalf of Tolya Rodin. They had a big ask. They wanted Bonafide to perform an assassination.

A major one.

Perhaps Noah's ego had gotten away with him. He was convinced that, between the techniques he had developed for MK Ultra, a heavy cocktail of pharmaceuticals, and some new tricks he had put together, he could twist the man's mind enough that he would indeed *want* to kill the President of the United States.

Except that wasn't what had happened. At all. Jack Bonafide was strangely resilient. It quickly became obvious that he was not going to go along with Noah's plans at all. The good doctor continued hammering away at him, but Jack Bonafide was a rock that could not be broken. Then Arkady had revealed that Bonafide was a former member of Delta Force.

Fortunately, Arkady had taken Doctor Barrister up on his suggestion of bringing in an alternate. Sid Felton was the perfect tool for something like this. He had been easy to break, had military experience, and was a legitimate patient from the working wing of the hospital.

There was a loud knocking at the door, and Noah knew right away it was Grunewald. The orderly didn't seem to know his own strength and was incapable of knocking softly, despite Noah's repeated admonishments.

"Enter," Noah said and slid the briefcase under his desk, out of sight.

The door opened and Grunewald entered.

"Is he ready?" Noah asked.

"He is," Grunewald replied. "We have a safe-house set up for him to operate out of. He's got money, clothes, and some of the basics."

"The basics?" Noah asked.

"Suppressed pistol, sniper rifle, you know," Grunewald said, smiling. "The basics."

Noah looked at his watch and sighed.

"It's been a good ride, my friend," he said. "But I think our hours here are numbered."

"They're prepping Bonafide for one more fight," Grunewald said. "Do we let it go ahead?"

"Yes," Noah replied. "But afterward, take him to Sub-Basement C and shoot him in the back of the head."

"What will I do?" Grunewald asked. There was real concern on his face.

"What do you mean?"

"What I mean is I don't want to end up back in Central America taking pot shots at revolutionaries. I like it here. I like what we are achieving."

Noah paused to consider it.

"Have you ever thought about private contracting?" Noah asked.

"What do you mean?"

Noah dug into his pocket and handed Grunewald a card.

"Meet me at that address in a few hours. I'll have something for you."

"What about the Agency?" Grunewald asked.

"I have a sneaking suspicion," Noah said, "that after today, the Agency will no longer have much use for men like us."

CHAPTER 3

An Undisclosed Location
Washington D.C.
March 20, 1981

TOLYA RODIN SWITCHED on the lamp and sighed. He looked around the room he was sequestered in. It was nice enough, with mahogany bookcases, antique furniture, a leather couch, and a fully stocked wet bar. The marble floor had radiant heating, and soft music played from a speaker system built into the ceiling.

Still, it was underground, and—at least, for the moment—it had become his prison.

The logbook was still out there. Yahontov remained missing after being taken into custody by the CIA. Either one of these had the potential to out him, and if this were to be the case, it was important that he not be found. Until both of those wild cards were secured, Tolya would stay in hiding, only occasionally venturing out when important business demanded it of him.

He had made one such exception for the meeting with Kelvin, but that had been a one-time deal. Tolya believed that Kelvin would follow through and, once again, attempt to secure the logbook. He wondered, however, whether Kelvin had really believed Tolya's promise to make him the Governor of New York. The whole idea made no logical sense, yet Kelvin had readily bought into it. He had believed the lie because he wanted to.

The music wafting from the recessed speaker was Yevstigney Fomin's *Orfey i Evridika*. It was a famous Russian melodramatic opera, and while Tolya did not care much for the themes, it did remind him of a simpler time. A time when kings and tsars ruled the world. Many looked back on this age with scorn and derided it as being tyrannical, but Tolya believed that those people viewed the world through naive eyes.

Simplicity such as that, handed down by these supposed tyrants of history, was needed once again. People—particularly the Americans—had far too much freedom, and it was costing them more than they could possibly know. They just lacked the eyes to see it.

The time for kings and tsars, though, was long gone. Tolya understood this. But who could replace them?

Corporations.

Corporate rule could prove to be the most effective in all of history, because not only would the capitalist nations and their citizens willingly accept it, but they would stand in line for it. They would fork out their hard-earned money for it.

The door unlatched, and Tolya turned toward the sound. There was only one person it could possibly be—only one person who knew where he was—so he greeted Arkady Radovich with a nod and a smile. He had been quite lucky in his acquisition of the former Alpha Group commander, a man who had once been sent to kill him but was now his indomitable right hand.

Arkady closed the door behind himself and then tested the latch. Despite the fact that no one aside from the contractors who had built the space even knew it existed, Arkady was ever the perfectionist.

"How did it go?" Tolya asked.

"Better than expected," Arkady replied.

"Was Bonafide turned?"

"No," Arkady said.

Tolya's confusion was obvious.

"Then how could it have gone 'better than expected?'"

"I never thought Doctor Barrister would turn Jack Bonafide," Arkady said. "I understand it is what you wanted, the agent beyond suspicion who could get close enough to the President to do the deed, but what we have secured instead will be just as effective."

Tolya took the bait.

"And what would that be?"

"Another agent. Also with military training, albeit not to Mister Bonafide's level. However, it was that very training which was making Bonafide such a tough nut to crack."

"This other man?" Tolya asked. "When will he be ready?"

"The wheels are already in motion."

Tolya looked around the room.

"I modeled this place after my father's study, you

know," Tolya said, and he began preparing himself a drink. "He was a Party member. Very powerful. He could easily have spared me government service, but he chose not to."

Tolya seemed to think about this for a moment and then pulled a second glass from the cabinet. This meant something, and Arkady knew it. Tolya had never prepared him a drink before.

"Why is that?" Arkady asked. "Did you wish to be spared?"

"No, I suppose not," Tolya said with a shrug. "But it is the thought, you understand? Perhaps my lot would have been different, had he not directly volunteered me for the Directorate S program."

Tolya finished preparing the drinks and crossed the small room, handing the second glass to Arkady.

"What of your own father?" Tolya asked. "You never talk about yourself."

"I did not think it was part of the job."

"It isn't," Tolya said. "But perhaps we are past that now."

"I killed him," Arkady said, "and fed his remains to wild dogs in the Siberian forest."

This clearly took Tolya aback.

"I have asked too much," Tolya said. "I did not mean to pry."

"It matters not," Arkady said. "He was cruel to my mother. When I was big enough, I struck him with a cast iron pan and finished the job with a kitchen knife. The dogs delivered his remains to the soil."

"You loved your mother," Tolya surmised.

Arkady cocked his head to the side and looked at Tolya quizzically.

"No," Arkady said. "She was equally cruel, but she was the more shrewd of the two. When I was very young and my father was at work at the rail yard, she took me aside in the kitchen and demanded my pledge of loyalty. I gave it. Love is a withering thing, Tolya, that can never stand up against the trials of time and the wicked heart of man. Loyalty, though? Loyalty is forever."

Tolya held out his glass in a toast.

"To loyalty," Tolya said.

Arkady clinked his glass with Tolya's and took a sip. He smiled. It was a fine vodka.

"How long will you be down here, do you think?" Arkady asked.

"Only as long as it takes for an assassin's bullet to fly, my friend. Once one of the most powerful nations in the world is mourning its fallen leader, I will no longer be of much concern."

. . .

Saint Elizabeth's Mental Hospital
Washington D.C.
March 20, 1981

"You know, Jack is really fast at picking locks," Carrie said as she glanced around the parking lot.

Mac, in the process of picking the lock, looked up from where he was kneeling beside the side entrance.

"Thanks," Mac said.

"Yeah," Clark said. "Like, crazy fast. One minute you'd be saying 'Hey, Jack, I wonder what's behind that door,' and then, all of a sudden, he's inside."

"Do either of you want to do this?" Mac barked.

It took a few more moments for them all to hear the resonant click of the lock. Mac stood, smiled smugly, and then eased the door open.

The interior of the hospital was a washed-out apocalyptic grey, courtesy of the paint on the walls and the flickering overhead lights. Mac closed the door behind them until it latched and then waited for his eyes to adjust to the dim light.

"Does any of this look familiar?" Carrie asked.

"We came down this hallway, I think. I'm pretty sure the room I was in is to the left, but I think it was a morgue of some kind."

"This sounds like a line out of a bad horror movie," Clark said, "but I think we should split up. There's just too much ground to cover."

"You're right, that *does* sound like a line out of a horror movie, but it's the only option we've got." Carrie checked her watch. "There's no way this should take more than fifteen minutes, so we'll meet back here then."

"Let's sync our watches," Mac said, pulling back his shirt sleeve to reveal his Timex.

"I don't have a watch like that," Clark said. "A wristwatch, I mean."

"What are you talking about?" Mac asked.

Clark reached into his pocket and retrieved a pocket watch on a long chain.

"I have one of these."

"Okay," Mac said. "Well, you meet us back here in eighteen ninety-seven or wherever the fuck you found that thing."

. . .

Jack stood in front of the thick steel door that lead into the padded room and waited while one of the orderlies unlocked it. Was he going to look across the room and see Yahontov on the other side? Jack looked over his shoulder at Foster.

"You can stop this any time," Jack said in a low voice.

He was attempting to communicate with Foster without the other two men overhearing.

"I wouldn't want to," Foster said. "Unlike you, I believe in what we're doing here. In time, you'll learn."

Jack turned back to the doorway. There was no point in trying to reason with the man. Foster may not have been as fanatical as the others, but he was evidently still a supporter.

Another orderly opened the heavy door, and Jack watched as it swung open. The door across the room was still closed, so he could not yet see his adversary. Foster moved to inject Jack with adrenaline.

"I don't need it," Jack said.

"You're doped up on Thorazine," Foster countered.

Jack knew he wouldn't be able to keep his wits about him with the adrenaline surging through his system, so he decided to take a risk. He turned and shoved Foster across the hallway. The big man slammed into the wall.

Jesus, Jack thought. *That took about all the strength I've got.*

"Leave me the fuck alone!" Jack shouted.

Foster kept his composure, stood up, and straightened his jacket out.

"Fine," he said. "Have it your way." He turned to the other orderly. "Make a note to up Bonafide's dose of Thorazine."

Jack stepped into the padded room and heard the door slam shut behind him.

At the same time, the door across the room opened and, sure enough, in stepped Yahontov.

Shit, Jack thought. *The last time I saw this guy, it was dark. He's a hell of a lot bigger than I remember.*

Yahontov clearly recognized Jack.

"*You,*" Yahontov said quietly.

Jack looked over his shoulder to where the door behind him had closed, then across the room past Yahontov. His door was shut as well, but Jack could see a man looking through the Plexiglas at him.

"I don't have time to explain this," Jack said. "But if you want to get out of this alive, you need to trust me."

"*Trust* you?" Yahontov asked. "Why in the hell would I trust *you?*"

"Because, whether you like it or not, I saved your life, you son of a bitch! I could have let you die in that hallway lickety-split, but I kept you alive." Jack looked over his shoulder again and then back to Yahontov. "The longer we stand here jawin', the more likely they are to know something's up. Are you with me? I'm your only way out of this."

Yahontov stared at Jack for a moment and then charged forward.

Jack took that to be a firm "yes."

Mac stopped in the corridor and looked around. Nothing was familiar. He was starting to think that splitting up had been a bad idea.

He hadn't been given much time to think about his situation. In fact, he hadn't really been alone since he had first left this place with Daniel. Now, he wondered whether that was what he needed. Just a little time alone to put everything together.

Daniel's comment about him being dead in a year kept cycling through his head. Was that really true? She had said it wasn't necessarily a sure thing, but he had the feeling the odds of him making it past the year mark were pretty damn slim. Was there something he needed to do before then? Something he needed to accomplish or put to rest to tie everything up and make his life mean something?

Yes, he thought to himself. *Help Jack get out of this hellhole.*

"Who in the hell are you?" a voice called out.

Mac turned and saw a man standing at the end of the hallway. He was larger than Mac—which took some doing—and looked like he had some German blood in him.

"The Maytag repairman," Mac said. "I heard your washers are fucked up."

Grunewald stared at Mac Bonafide for a moment and then pulled a collapsible baton from his pocket and extended it to its full length.

"Friend," Grunewald said, "you just walked into the wrong building."

Clark wiped his hands against his shirt and then stopped to look down at them. He was sweating.

He didn't have a weapon. That thought instantly became the loudest in his head. Scarn had given him a .38 back at the house, but he had left it in the car.

You don't have a weapon, he thought. *Why in the hell aren't you armed?*

"Because I'm an analyst on leave from the Agency," Clark said aloud.

He stopped and looked around, then breathed a sigh of relief. No one had heard him talking to himself.

In that moment, he heard something. Voices murmuring in the semi-darkness. A door opened to his left. Clark's hand instinctively went for the gun that wasn't there.

"Are you the instructor?"

Clark stared at the man who had opened the door. He was dressed in a suit and wearing a stethoscope around his neck. His name tag read: *Dr. Richards.* Behind him was a classroom full of other Doctors, and scrawled on the blackboard were the words: "Advances in Neuroscience— 1981".

Clark knew he was trapped. If he said he was not the instructor they would quickly begin asking who he was and what he was doing there.

"Yep," Clark said with a smile. "That's me."

Carrie stopped at the end of the hallway and read the name on the door: *Doctor Barrister.*

She remembered that name. Daniel had mentioned it. Barrister was the one running this madhouse.

Carrie reached out and turned the doorknob. It wasn't locked. She retracted her hand and pushed the door open with her foot.

Doctor Barrister looked up from his desk.

"What are you doing here?" he asked. "You're not supposed to be here."

Jack dropped to a half-kneeling position, clashed with Yahontov, and then suplexed the bigger man, flipping him over and down onto the floor hard enough that it knocked the wind out of the Russian. Jack then spun around and took his back, getting his hooks into his hips and flattening him out.

"Be ready!" Jack hissed. "Pretend you're out."

Jack snaked his arms around Yahontov to form a rear naked choke. He began applying pressure, and the big man felt his head becoming light.

"That... won't be hard," Yahontov said.

Then he went limp.

Jack stood up and looked down at the body and back to the door. It clicked open, and one of the orderlies walked in, brandishing his cattle prod. Jack recognized him as a man named Vega.

"Is he dead?" Vega called out, pointing the cattle prod at Jack.

"As a fucking doornail," Jack said.

"Hmph," Vega grunted.

Foster and the third orderly were close behind their associate.

Vega knelt down to check Yahontov's pulse.

Jack knew he didn't have much strength left in him, so he was going to have to make this one count. He stepped forward and swung a football kick hard enough to put the old pigskin between the goal posts at Texas High, cracking Vega's skull and sending him ass over teakettle.

Yahontov lunged toward Vega, grabbed the cattle prod, and then jumped to his feet, slamming it into the chest of the third orderly. The man's body went rigid, and Jack swore he could see the fillings in his teeth lighting up.

Yahontov released him and swung the cattle prod toward Foster.

"No!" Jack shouted, holding out a hand.

Yahontov stopped.

"He did right by me," Jack said.

Yahontov smiled like he was looking at a dim

child and then slammed the cattle prod into the side of Foster's neck, triggering it until the orderly fell to the floor.

"I'm not going to let your weakness get me killed," Yahontov said.

The opposite door began to rattle as the orderlies worked the lock, so there was no time for debate.

"Move!" Jack shouted.

Jack grabbed Yahontov by the arm and pushed him through the open door that he had entered through.

Jack slammed the door behind him and worked the lock. As a safety measure, it could not be unlocked from inside the cell, so he knew that they were safe from the orderlies attempting to enter from the other side.

"Okay," Jack said. "We—"

Jack felt electricity coursing through his body as Yahontov hit him with the cattle prod, and then he fell to the floor.

Mac picked Grunewald up and slammed him into the wall, hard enough that the plaster cracked. The German was stronger than hell, even for Mac Bonafide. It had occurred to Mac that neither one knew the other, or even why he was there, but they were both clearly wired the same: default aggressive.

Grunewald slammed his fist into Mac's ribs several times, causing the big Texan to loosen his grip and step back to catch his breath.

Grunewald started moving forward, and Mac took advantage of the small hallway. He turned, braced himself against the wall, and threw the hardest mule kick he could, right into Grunewald's sternum. There was an audible *crack*, and the German fell heavily to the floor, the contact with the ground dislocating his left shoulder.

"Stay down!" Mac shouted.

Grunewald made a move to get up, and Mac drew his pistol. He stepped forward and pressed the muzzle against the man's head.

"Did I fucking stutter?" Mac growled.

Grunewald froze and slowly held his hands up.

"On your face, now!" Mac said.

Grunewald complied and rolled over onto the floor. Mac zip-tied his hands behind his back and stood back up.

"We work for the same people," Grunewald said.

"The hell we do," Mac said. "I work for Uncle Sam and the state of Texas, in that order."

Grunewald smiled.

"New guy, huh?" Grunewald asked. "You'll figure it out soon enough. We play in a house of mirrors, friend. Sooner or later, we all look the same."

"Why am I not supposed to be here?" Carrie asked.

She kept her pistol trained on Doctor Barrister. While she did not know him personally, she had heard enough from Daniel to understand he could not be trusted.

Barrister looked at his watch and then back to Carrie.

"You don't understand what you're doing," Barrister said.

"Where's Jack?" Carrie demanded, having decided not to get pulled into this man's mind games.

"Jack?" Barrister asked, obviously confused. "Wait... are you talking about Bonafide?"

"Yes!" Carrie said. She stepped forward and pulled back the hammer on her Beretta 1951.

"Who is he?" Barrister asked, relaxing his posture. "He's quite an interesting man. We couldn't break him, no matter how much pressure I applied. I know about his service with Delta, but not much beyond that."

"What did you do to him?"

"It doesn't matter," Barrister replied. "By now, he should be dead."

"You son of a bitch!" Carrie shouted. She took another step toward the doctor and then

felt her body seize up. She dropped to the floor like a ton of bricks.

"Thank you," Barrister said.

The orderly lowered his cattle prod and nodded.

CIA Headquarters
Langley, VA
March 20, 1981

"He's been looking for you," Eleanor Babbitt said as Michael Scarn entered the outer office of the Director of the CIA.

"I was held up," Scarn replied. "D.C. traffic."

Eleanor raised an eyebrow.

"What?" Scarn asked.

"He opened the sealed envelopes."

"What sealed envelopes?" Scarn asked, then realized what she meant. "He wasn't supposed to do that."

"I know."

"How many did he open?"

"All of them."

Michael Scarn was an encyclopedia of Central Intelligence Agency lore, which made sense for a man who had dreamed of working for the CIA ever since he was a young boy. His fascination with the Agency had been born after his father had told him about the adventures of the OSS during World War Two, an organization that would later go on to become the CIA.

It wasn't until Scarn became a supervisory agent that he had first heard about the supposed "sealed files" that were passed down from one Director to the next. The brief was that the files were never to be opened, as knowledge of the contents would cause more chaos than it would solve.

It figured that Tresham would be the first Director to open all of them.

Scarn walked to the main door of the inner office and let out a breath. He turned the knob and entered.

Mike Tresham looked up from his desk.

"I know you're a giant nerd about this kind of stuff," Tresham said by way of a greeting, holding up a file that Scarn took to be one from the "sealed" stack. "So, I assume you knew about these?"

"I knew the rumors," Scarn said. "But I didn't know they existed for a fact until just now."

"Jesus Christ, Scarn!" Tresham shouted. "This is a *goddamn* mess!"

Michael Scarn turned and closed the door. He knew that Eleanor Babbitt had a reputation for thinking she was somehow part of the official hierarchy of the CIA leadership, but he planned on disabusing her of that notion ASAP. He valued her experience and her counsel, but her "need to know" had its limits.

"What are we looking at?" Scarn asked.

"A monkey fucking a football, as near as I can tell."

Scarn held up a hand.

"Take a breath," Scarn said. "*Sir.*"

Tresham was ready to snap at his subordinate, but then he took a breath and relaxed. He knew Scarn was right, and that was why he had retained the man as his right hand. While Tresham had not had any qualms about assaulting a suspect in FBI Headquarters, he knew that Scarn would have tried a different approach, and that was what he needed.

He needed a counterpoint to his aggression, not another "yes man."

"What are we looking at?" Scarn repeated the question.

"Apparently, we're running an off-book wet works shop out of Saint Elizabeth's Mental Hospital."

Shit, Scarn thought to himself. *This is going to be bad.*

Tresham picked up on the shift in Scarn's demeanor and walked around his desk.

"What do you know?" Tresham asked.

Saint Elizabeth's Mental Hospital
Washington D.C.
March 20, 1981

"Wake up!" Mac shouted, slapping his brother hard across the face.

Jack opened his eyes and focused his vision. He looked Mac Bonafide in the eyes.

"Heaven or hell?" Jack asked.

"What?" Mac asked.

"Are we in heaven or hell?"

"We're in Washington D.C.," Mac replied as he pulled his brother to his feet. "So, you kind of split the difference, I guess."

Jack braced himself against the wall and looked around. He was still in the hospital. He looked back at Mac and studied him for a moment. He could feel his own surge of natural adrenaline had cleared most of the Thorazine out of his system, and he was starting to feel normal again.

"I don't understand," Jack said. "You were dead."

"I was sober once, too," Mac said. "Things change. I'll explain later, but for now, we need to get the hell out of here."

Carrie rolled over onto her back and looked up at the ceiling.

She felt as if she had been hit by a truck. Then she remembered what had happened. She sat bolt upright and went for the pistol that wasn't there.

"Son of a bitch!"

Carrie leapt to her feet and darted out into the hallway, but then lost control of her legs and slammed into the wall, falling ass over teakettle. She had not quite gained full motor control of her limbs after being electrocuted and was now painfully aware of the fact.

She looked down at the floor and saw her pistol. It must have flown out of her hand into the hallway when she fell. She scooped it up and could feel that it had been unloaded.

"Come on!" she heard a familiar voice shouting.

Carrie turned and saw Mac guiding Jack down the hallway.

"Am I glad to see you two!" Carrie said, limping forward to join the two brothers. "Where the hell is Clark?"

"Smokin' cigarettes and watching *Captain Kangaroo* for all I know," Mac said. "He probably got out already."

"We have to find Clark!" Carrie insisted.

Mac let out a sigh.

"Look, if he isn't in the car, I'll come back or him. But for now, we need to get Jack out of here."

"So, as you can see," Clark said, "we are making great strides in our understanding not only of how the human brain works but specifically how it uses prediction to optimize survivability in a chaotic world. We see this in how we apply Bayesian theory to neurology."

Clark caught movement out of the corner of his eye and saw Mac, Carrie and Jack running through the parking lot.

"Oh," he said and turned back to the classroom of psychiatrists. "Does anyone know how to unlock this window?"

Still lacking fine motor control, Carrie fumbled the car keys on her first attempt, then snatched them up from the ground and unlocked the car.

Jack slid into the back seat and looked across at the unconscious David Kelvin.

"Is that the Attorney General?" Jack asked.

"*Former* Attorney General," Carrie corrected him.

"What the hell have you two been up to?"

"Aside from saving your ass?" Mac asked. "Kidnapping, attempted murder. The usual."

"Don't leave!" Clark shouted as he ran across the parking lot.

Jack smiled.

"Figures," he said lazily.

"He never gave up looking for you," Mac said. "That means something."

"I know."

Clark ran the last few hundred feet to the car and jumped into the back seat.

Carrie fired up the engine and was about to throw the car into gear when a beeping emitted from the glove box.

"It's the brick phone," Mac said, using his nickname for the giant cellular phone they had been given.

"Well, answer it," Carrie said.

Mac reached into the front, opened the glove box, and pulled out the bulky device. He elongated the antenna and hit the call button.

"Frank's Morgue. You stack 'em, we pack 'em."

"Holy shit!" Tresham said from the other end of the line. "It's true! You're fucking alive?"

Mac turned to Carrie and said quietly, "*Fuck!* It's Tresham."

"I can still hear you, asshole!" Tresham shouted.

Mac grimaced and then placed the phone back to his ear. "Yes, sir, I'm alive. Carrie, too."

"What the fuck?" Carrie snapped.

"Like he didn't know," Mac growled.

"Hey!' Tresham barked. "Abbot and Costello! Get on point!"

"Yes, sir," Mac replied.

"You two assholes need to come in. I'll organize a safe house where you'll be met by Scarn."

"Sir, we have Jack."

"*What?* Where'd you find him? Was he in Saint Elizabeth's?"

"Yes, sir."

"*Jesus*," Tresham groaned. "We're in the process of shutting that place down, so don't worry about them." Tresham clearly hesitated. "I don't even want to ask, but are you currently near anyone who used to work directly for the President of the United States?"

"You mean Kelvin? He's passed out in the backseat."

"Mac, you really need to work on the fine art of subtlety."

The phone went dead. Mac looked at it for a moment and then stowed it back in the glovebox.

"Well," Mac said, "I guess we have our orders."

Carrie started the engine and pulled the car forward, then set off down the winding road.

Clark leaned forward from the back seat to look at something in the distance ahead of them.

"Who's that?" he asked.

Mac also leaned forward.

"It's a man running," he said.

Carrie accelerated until they caught up with him. He was wearing a patient's uniform similar to Jack and was running at a dead sprint down the road. Carrie slowed the car to keep pace with him, and Mac leaned out the window.

"Nice day for it," Mac called out.

Yahontov turned to look at him and then returned to his running.

"Isn't that Yahontov?" Clark asked, turning to Jack.

"Who the hell is Yahontov?" Carrie asked.

"He was part of the assault group that hit HQ last month," Clark replied.

"What do you know about that?" Mac said, and he leaned back out the window. "Hey there, Yahtzee or whatever the hell your name is. Why don't you stop running and get in the trunk? We ain't got time for this."

Yahontov carried on running.

Mac drew his pistol and waved it casually out the window.

"If you don't stop running, I'm going to shoot you in the back of the head," Mac called out.

Yahontov slowed his pace and then stopped.

Carrie stopped the car and popped the trunk.

Robard's Halfway House
Washington D.C.
March 20, 1981

Sid stopped in the poorly lit hallway and looked down at his feet. He was still wearing his hospital issue slippers. Everything else was different, but that one thing remained the same. They were dirty from his walk through the D.C. streets, but all the same, he thought he might keep them. Perhaps just as a reminder of where he had been.

Everything else about him spoke to where he was going. His clothes were simple but effective, allowing him to mix with the crowd and become the proverbial "gray man." In his left hand, he held a garbage bag stuffed with clothes, some food, and a single book.

The book was a copy of George Orwell's *1984*. Doctor Barrister had given it to him as a teaching tool. The book had helped Sid to understand the role of the Thought Police in the suppression of free will and the warping of the American mind. Ironically, the American government itself was the Thought Police. The very apparatus that was supposed to be leading the American people out of the darkness was instead enshrouding them in it.

He set down the case that he carried in his right hand. It contained the Czech made sniper rifle he had been given by Foster. At first, Sid had been unsure about the weapon, because it was a hell of a lot different from the M-14 he had used overseas. Foster had assured him that it was a "damn fine weapon" and would get the job done. As a sidearm, Sid had a .38 revolver stuffed into his waistband. He wasn't exactly sure what he would need to complete his mission, so he had been given a little of everything.

Sid dug into his pocket and found the key that he had been given at the front desk. He worked it in the lock and opened the door to what was a small studio apartment. In truth, it barely even qualified as that. It was a single room, perhaps one hundred feet by one hundred feet, with a sink in the corner. The sink was actually something of a luxury for a place like this, as the communal washroom was one floor below.

Despite its lack of creature comforts, Robard's

Halfway House was the perfect place for a man like Sid; the perfect place for a man who did not want to be found.

Sid closed the door and locked the two dead-bolts. As he did so, he wondered whether they were meant to guard against intruders or just the other residents.

He looked around the room and let out a breath. He was home. This was home. He dropped his garbage bag on the metal frame bed and opened it up. From inside, he pulled out a photograph and a piece of tape. Sid walked over to the wall and taped the photo to it. He made sure to put it in a place where a casual observer looking from the doorway would not notice it.

He returned to the bag and rummaged around for a moment before he found the red felt-tip pen. He uncapped it and walked back to the photo. He whistled the dwarves theme song from the Disney movie *Snow White* as he crossed out the eyes of the person in the photo.

"He'll be drawing flies soon."

East German Secret Police Detachment Zero
Leipzig, East Germany
March 20, 1981

Wilhelm Fischer did his best to ignore the minder, but it was difficult.

The man had been tasked to shadow him ever since Wilhelm had arrived at the airport in East Berlin. The travel had been no easy task, moving through Canada under false documents before eventually flying into Poland and then again into East Germany. It also didn't help that he was now on Interpol's "Most Wanted" list.

It was his first trip back to the Motherland.

Granted, he had been receiving materiel and logistical support from the East German government for years, but being there in person was different. In one fell swoop, he had a more acute understanding of just what he was fighting for. It wasn't just about the white race or about so-called "hate." No, it was about heritage. It was about pride. Now that he was finally walking amongst his brethren once more, he could see that.

East Germany—and Leipzig, in particular—was austere, no question about it. That was what Wilhelm liked about it. There was no fat. The place and the people were lean. They were ready for battle.

"He'll see you now."

Wilhelm turned to the clerk and nodded. He had been waiting in the hallway for an hour to see a man who, by all reports, was a living legend.

Heinrich Weber was one of the true old breed. He had been an SS man in counterintelligence during World War Two, making the transition into the East German Secret Police after the war. Nothing was officially reported, but word through the grapevine suggested he had been running secret missions on behalf of the East German government ever since. His primary mission was to destabilize Israel and allow the Arabs to push it into the ocean.

Wilhelm walked across the perfectly polished tile floor into the small office and shut the door behind him.

"I'm glad you made the trip," Heinrich said with a smile.

He stood up from his desk and thrust out his hand. It was almost an attack. Wilhelm shook it and tried not to stare at the man's prosthetic nose, unavoidably wondering about the story behind it. He recalled a man from his youth that he had seen only a few times during his time with the Nazi leader Jurgen Steiner. He wondered if it could possibly be the same man.

"I'm glad to be here," Wilhelm replied.

"Have a seat," Heinrich said.

Wilhelm sat in the offered chair. It was simple but well-crafted, much like most of East Germany seemed to be.

"I'm ready," Wilhelm said.

"Ready?" Heinrich asked. "What do you mean?"

"For the next step."

Heinrich drummed his fingers on the table and smiled.

"But you just got here. Wouldn't you like to... see

the sights?"

"I failed," Wilhelm said. "On all fronts. I seek only a chance to redeem myself. Nothing more."

"I see," Heinrich replied. "We can give you that opportunity, but how far are you willing to take it?"

"I don't understand the question."

Heinrich smiled. He understood what Wilhelm was implying. There was no limit to what he was willing to do.

"What casualty rate is acceptable to you?" Heinrich followed up.

"As many as it takes."

"That sounds awfully callous, don't you think?" Heinrich asked. "We're talking about human lives here. Real people with families."

Wilhelm leaned back in his chair.

"They are not *my* people," he said. "I only care about my people; those who are, right now, being trampled by the same 'real people with families' that you speak of. They are fighting as close to a Holy War as America will ever see, and just last month, dozens of them were murdered by federal agents who invaded my home. Those were also 'real people with families.' So, no, Herr Weber, I do not care how many of the enemy I kill to bring about a new world order."

Heinrich narrowed his eyes at Wilhelm for a moment, primarily trying to assess if the man was just full of bluster, or if he was truly as willing as he seemed to embrace the darkness.

"Anthrax," Heinrich said.

Wilhelm sat upright in his chair and leaned forward.

"Where?" Wilhelm asked.

"Los Angeles."

Wilhelm tried to hold back his smile but was unable.

"I believe I could put together a team to deploy it," Wilhelm said.

"No," Heinrich replied and shook his head. "It has to be you. Only you. This is very hard to get, and it must be done right. We have other vials that are to be deployed by other teams, but yours will be the tip of the spear."

"I know that you don't doubt my willingness to prosecute the mission," Wilhelm said. "But it seems like I would need help with something like this."

"We have a dispersal device in place on the Paul Hastings Tower in City Nation Plaza, one of the tallest buildings in the city. All you will have to do is insert the canister, set the timer, and then make your departure."

"Why me?" Wilhelm asked. "I'm happy to do it, of course, but why not one of your other agents?"

"Because just before you release the agent into the city, you will drop off a tape at the local news station taking full responsibility." Heinrich held Wilhelm's gaze for a moment. "You will go down as the greatest mass murderer in American history, and they will know that it was one of their own who brought them to their knees."

Wilhelm thought about it for a moment and then nodded.

"Justice," he said. "That's what it sounds like to me."

"You know," Heinrich said, "I've been watching you for a very long time, Wilhelm. Even before Attica."

Wilhelm studied Heinrich for a moment.

"It was you, wasn't it?" Wilhelm asked.

"Do you remember?" Heinrich asked.

"I do," Wilhelm said.

Heinrich Weber and Jurgen Steiner had been the men responsible for training Wilhelm as a young boy and unleashing him on the school he attacked. The very same attack that would garner him a lengthy prison sentence.

"You suffered much because of what we did and

because of who we taught you to be. How do you feel about that?"

Wilhelm paused for a moment and then felt a wetness in his eyes. In that moment, he realized that this was as close as he would ever come to meeting his father in his adult life.

"Grateful," Wilhelm replied.

Heinrich smiled.

"There is just one detail," he said. He reached beneath his desk, retrieved a bag, and handed it to Wilhelm. "That contains everything you will need. You are to do nothing until you receive confirmation directly from me."

Wilhelm took the bag.

"Is there a chance it won't happen?" Wilhelm asked.

"Unlikely," Heinrich replied, shaking his head. "But our resources are not what they once were, and we are relying on an outside benefactor to finance this operation. I am only waiting for his phone call to transfer the necessary funds so that we can complete the operation."

"Who is it?" Wilhelm asked.

Heinrich smiled.

"You wouldn't believe me if I told you."

CHAPTER 4

A CIA Safehouse
Washington D.C.
March 20, 1981

CARRIE PARKED the car and stared out the windshield for a moment. She shook her head.

"What is it?" Mac asked.

"This is wrong," Carrie said.

"Jack's on drugs, Mac's alive and the Attorney General of the United States is passed out and drooling on my shoulder!" Clark blurted. "Nothing about this damn operation has been right."

"No, I mean this safehouse," Carrie continued. "I

just don't like it. How did we go so fast from operating in the dark to coming back into the light?"

"It's a leap of faith, Carrie. We're short on options and long on threat. Even after what Tresham told us, we still don't know what kind of blowback we're looking at from that place. I don't think that Doctor Barrister is going to take what we did to his people lying down."

Mac looked at Carrie's pensive expression. "Tell the truth," he said. "Are you still raw about Tresham burning you on that deal?"

Carrie thought about it for a moment.

"Maybe. Maybe that's it."

"We don't know the details of how that went down," Mac said. "Tresham has always seemed like a straight shooter. We need to give him the benefit of the doubt."

Jack groaned from the back seat. He had passed out during the car ride and had been drifting in and out of consciousness ever since.

"How's he doing?" Carrie asked.

Mac turned in his seat to at Jack.

"Not good," he said. "He's in a bad way."

Jack's breathing sped up, and he clutched his chest. He sat bolt upright.

"Shit," he hissed.

"What is it?" Clark asked.

"Heart attack," Jack said. "I'm having a fucking *heart attack!*"

"No!" Mac said firmly. "You're not! It's the drugs! It's the old shit coming back."

"It's real!" Jack shouted.

He turned and worked the door handle, then spilled out onto the street. His lungs were going a hundred miles per hour. He dropped to his hands and knees and emptied the contents of his stomach.

By now, everyone was out of the car.

Carrie knelt down next to Jack.

"Get your breathing under control, Jack," she soothed. "Slow it down. Slow it down."

"I can't!" Jack countered. "I can't do it!"

The former Delta operator dropped into the fetal position and tried to press his face into the coolness of the concrete. Something about it felt calming; felt safe.

"They're going to... they're going to kill the president," Jack managed to get out.

"What in the hell did you say?" Carrie asked, the alarm in her voice obvious.

Jack pulled himself together enough to look up and lock eyes with Carrie.

"They're going to kill the President of the United States."

Clark looked around. No one had seen them yet.

"We can't do this here," Clark said. "We have to move him. *Now!*"

Mac looked around and then nodded.

"He's right. Let's get him in the safehouse."

As if on cue, a door down the block opened, and Scarn stepped out onto the street.

"You four!" he shouted. "Get in here!"

Mac and Carrie tried to pick Jack up off the ground, but he resisted, shoving Carrie away and dropping to a knee. He placed his hands on the side of his head and winced. Mac reached out to grab him, but Jack countered with a palm heel strike to his ribs.

Mac stepped back and looked at Carrie, then back to Jack as the man stumbled to his feet.

"Sorry as hell about this, brother, but we don't have this kind of time."

Mac stepped forward and threw a right hook, connecting with Jack's chin and putting him out like a light.

The Western Inn

Washington D.C.
March 20, 1981

Doctor Noah Barrister closed the door of the small motel room and set the lock. He paused for a moment in the darkness before reaching out and flicking on the single lamp in the room. A second light switch activated the dull fluorescents in the small changing room adjacent to the equally small bathroom.

He dropped his suitcase to the floor but held onto the steel briefcase full of cash. He crossed the room and dropped the case onto the lone full-size bed. He let out a breath and then turned to the mirror bolted to the wall over the dresser.

In the mirror, he saw an old man. He smiled at the old man, but the smile was forced. How had he gotten to this point? How had he lost so many years in the service of a cause that had benefitted him nothing? He had sacrificed his youth on the alter of patriotism, but to what end?

Noah turned to the briefcase full of money. Well, there was that, but its contents had nothing to do with his patriotism. He had secured that money by betraying the very thing he had sworn to protect. The question was not whether he regretted what he had done. He did not.

The real question was: would he do it one more time? Was it worth sticking his neck out just one more time for the biggest payday he would ever see?

Noah looked down at the phone on the dresser.

He knew the answer.

Yes, he would.

An Undisclosed Location
Washington D.C.
March 20, 1981

Arkady re-assembled the Colt 1911 .45 pistol and laid it on the mahogany table. It was not a weapon he had much experience with, as he had carried the standard issue Makarov pistol for most of his career, but he liked the feel of the Colt in his hand. It somehow felt more serious than the Makarov had, if that were possible. He smiled to himself, realizing that the thought in itself would have seemed heresy just a few months earlier.

142 / JORDAN VEZINA

The phone to his left rang, and Arkady frowned at being interrupted from his train of thought. He tested the weight of the pistol in his hand once more and then set it down. He picked up the phone but said nothing. He only waited.

"Are you there?" Noah Barrister asked.

"Yes," Arkady replied.

"The hospital is out of business."

"I see," Arkady said. "Are *we* still in business?"

"Yes. The agent has been deployed."

"Excellent."

"There's something else."

Arkady raised an eyebrow.

"I was under the impression this would mean our business was concluded," he said, the accusation in his voice clear.

"It is, but I am in a position to offer further support."

"And what would that be?"

"I had men working for me. They were masquerading as orderlies, but they are all experienced operators. Good men with solid track records in Central America and Vietnam. They can ensure that this operation goes off without a hitch."

"I see," Arkady said. "So... it seems that you are implying your man may fail."

"No, it's not that," Noah replied quickly. "I'm just saying it might be better if he has some backup. Some helpers to smooth the way."

"Meaning?" Arkady inquired.

"It might be best if you don't know."

"And you would provide this additional service free of charge?"

"Well—no," Noah replied, sounding flustered. "These things take time to develop. They cost money."

"How much money?"

"One million."

"Dollars?" Arkady asked.

"Of course," Noah replied curtly, sounding as if he had found his footing. "If you'd rather take your chances with just one man, that's your choice."

Arkady thought about the proposition for a moment. He had been authorized by Tolya Rodin to take any measures necessary to get the job done, and this seemed as though it would fall within those guidelines.

"I can authorize the additional payment," Arkady said, "so long as we have a guarantee. Some security, if you will."

"Security?" Noah asked.

"Yes," Arkady replied. "Your life. You will

144 / JORDAN VEZINA

deploy these additional men to shore up the one you have already dispatched. But if the President is still alive by this time next week, you will not be."

There was a pause on the line.

"Doctor Barrister?" Arkady asked. "Are we in agreement?"

"You'll pay my fee?" the doctor asked.

"It will be in your bank account by the end of the day."

"Cash," Noah said quickly. "I want cash."

"Fine," Arkady replied. "Cash it is. Do you agree to my terms?"

There was another pause.

"Yes," Noah said. "We are agreed."

A CIA Safehouse
Washington D.C.
March 20, 1981

"What in the hell is wrong with him?" Scarn asked, earning him a dirty look from Carrie.

"There's something wrong with his brain," Mac replied. "I've seen it before. Guys think they're having heart attacks; they get ringing in their ears; their hands shake."

"What causes it?" Scarn asked.

"Not really sure," Mac said. "Maybe combat. Jack had it under control before, but I think whatever has happened to him in that hospital has brought it back out again."

"There's something else," Carrie said. "Something he said right before Mac knocked him out."

"What is it?" Scarn asked.

"He said someone is going to kill the President."

"He's half out of his mind," Scarn replied. "Look at him!"

"You didn't see the look in his eyes!" Carrie snapped. "I did. This is serious."

Scarn examined her for a moment and then nodded.

"Okay, we're going to treat this as an actionable threat until we find out otherwise," Scarn said.

Jack was laid out on a cot in the large living room, and his eyes began to flutter.

"He's waking up," Clark said.

Jack pulled his body into a ball.

"Call... Angela," he said weakly. "Bethesda Naval Hospital. Angela Merril."

Jack pulled himself tighter into the fetal position, and his breathing increased rapidly.

"Shit," Mac spat. "He's freaking out again."

"Who in the hell is Angela Merril?" Carrie asked.

"I don't know," Clark replied. "But we better call Bethesda and track her down."

Be Here Now Yoga
Capitol Hill
Washington D.C.
March 20, 1981

Angela Merril sat on her mat and watched the members of her late afternoon class filter out the door. Despite becoming a fully-fledged respiratory therapist, she still taught at least a few classes a week in her old yoga studio because it was her passion. Unfortunately, the sessions had never quite paid the bills, and Angela had serious misgivings as to whether Yoga would ever catch on in America.

She looked at herself in the mirror across the room and tried to smile, but it looked fake. It figured, because Angela Merril understood that she *was* a fake. Any moment, someone was going to walk up behind her, tap her on the shoulder, and tell her that she didn't belong there teaching those people. They deserved better.

Angela thought the same thing each day at the Naval Hospital. At any moment, it would come.

Tap, tap.

"Excuse, Miss Merril? I think you know that you don't belong here, right? Aren't you embarrassed?"

She wasn't sure how she would react when the moment came, so she always tried to push it out of her head, but she knew that it would come all the same. It was just a matter of time.

She looked at herself in the mirror and examined the cute bob haircut she had gotten. At least, she had thought it would be cute. Now that she saw herself with it, she realized it was yet one more mask she was wearing, once again trying to be something she wasn't. Her thirty years had crept up on her and hit her like a hammer. She thought the bob haircut would make her look young again, but it didn't. Instead, it just made her look like a woman who didn't fully understand that she had entered her thirties.

Angela smiled, showing more teeth this time.

No, that was even worse. It was even more fake. She sighed and stood up from the floor, then began the work of rolling up her yoga mat. She could feel the thin layer of flesh covering her abdomen squishing together as she reached to the floor. She was getting fat.

"Angela?" a voice called out.

It was the girl at the front desk.

Angela turned and smiled, her bob haircut bouncing just as she had imagined it would. The deception was complete.

Angela stood in front of the door and looked up at the building. Was this real? The whole scenario seemed impossible to believe. She remembered Jack Bonafide from a little over two months prior. The handsome mystery man who couldn't breathe.

She suspected that he was some kind of CIA agent or Special Forces soldier, which made his dilemma even more amazing. This man could barely maintain a normal respiratory rhythm for more than a minute at a time when she'd met him. He lived in a constant state of either hyperventilation or apnea. His breathing had been either incredibly fast or not at all, yet he had been able to push his body beyond its limits over and over again for years.

As they had worked together on the respiratory exercises, she had watched his hard shell drift away like sand in the wind. It was very clear to her that there was something on his agenda, something he thought he needed to finish, but all the same, he had softened right before her eyes.

Then, suddenly, he was gone. She had harbored some fantasy that he might ask her out; that they might be together in some way. Then she had realized why that would never happen. He had seen through her, just like everyone else did. So, she had gone home to her studio apartment and sat in the darkness. Alone.

Now, it seemed that fate had stepped in. She reached out to knock on the door, but it opened abruptly. A woman stared at her. She was pretty enough, but she had a hard face and a sharp nose, and something in her eyes told Angela that she was not to be trifled with.

"Angela?" Carrie asked.

"Yes, ma'am," Angela said, her West Virginia twang surfacing, just as it always did in times of stress.

. . .

"Jack?" Angela asked as she walked into the room and saw him laid out on the cot.

She had not known why she had been summoned to the townhouse. She had only been told that it was in the interest of national security. Normally, even that would not have been enough to make her follow an order like this, but the fact that it came from Captain Mary Pritchard gave it a great deal more weight.

Jack turned his head to the side, his eyes half shut against what little light could be found in the room. He smiled weakly.

He looks horrible! she thought to herself. *Like he hasn't slept in weeks.*

"What happened to him?" Angela asked.

"As near as we can tell, for the past few weeks, his body has been pumped full of a mix of Thorazine, adrenaline, and God knows what else," Clark answered.

"My God!" Angela said with obvious alarm. "Why on earth would someone do that?"

"It's a long story," Carrie said. "But he asked for you specifically. His breathing is all messed up, and he can't seem to focus."

Angela knelt down beside the cot and set her medical bag on the floor. In addition to being a certified respiratory therapist, she had also been an EMT for nearly ten years. She retrieved a pen light and began checking Jack's pupils as she took his pulse.

"Jesus!" she said. "His resting heart rate is one twenty!"

"It's always like that," Mac replied, recalling the detail about his brother from when they were younger. Doctors had said that Jack's heart just ran fast.

"It's not supposed to be," Angela countered.

"Can you fix him?" Carrie pushed.

Angela looked in Jack's eyes for a moment before turning to Carrie.

"If I can get him back to Bethesda, get him checked in, and re-start his therapy, we might be able get him stable in a few days."

"By the end of the night," Scarn said, stepping forward.

"What?" Angela asked incredulously.

"I need him operational by the end of the night."

Angela stood up and went nose-to-nose with Scarn.

"I never said anything about *operational*! I said we *might* be able to get him stable. Emphasis on *might*."

"Someone is going to kill the President of the

United States," Scarn said flatly. Angela Merril's face changed. "Jack is the only one who can identify the assassin."

"You're serious," Angela said. It was a statement, not a question.

"Yes."

She looked at the floor and then back to Scarn.

"A professor of mine had a theory about how to quickly break someone out of a state like this."

"What is it?" Carrie asked.

"He called it the contrast method. The idea is to create a sympathetic nervous system overload and then force the subject to suppress it through breathing work and focus."

"How do you overload the sympathetic nervous system?" Clark asked.

Angela turned to him.

"A shot of adrenaline."

"He can't take more of that! His heart rate is already sky-high," Mac countered.

"I know!" Angela said. "That's why I don't want to do it. And it's not just one shot."

"How many?" Mac asked.

"As many as it takes."

"Is there any other way?" Scarn asked.

Angela thought for a moment.

"No."

"Then we have no choice," Scarn said.

"It could cause a stroke," Angela said. "He might die."

"Do it," Jack said quietly from the cot. "I wouldn't want to live like this, anyway."

Angela knelt down beside the cot.

"I'll do it as long as you understand the risks."

"I understand," Jack replied. "Now let's get it over with."

Mac crouched down and took his brother's hand.

"You hang in there, brother. You can do this."

"You know I will," Jack said. "If only so I can find out how in the hell you're still alive."

The Western Inn
Washington D.C.
March 20, 1981

Noah Barrister opened his eyes at the sound of the knock on his door. He wasn't sure if he had been asleep or just in some sort of deep meditation. If he

154 / JORDAN VEZINA

was honest about it, he wasn't certain if he ever really slept anymore.

When Noah Barrister closed his eyes, there was no such thing as sweet dreams; only a realm of shadows and sharp teeth.

He sat up and looked toward the door. Every muscle in his body had snapped from relaxation to being as taut as a wire.

"Who is it?" he asked.

"Grunewald," the familiar voice answered.

Noah relaxed a bit and stood up. He walked across the room and unlocked both the deadbolt and the chain lock.

He opened the door and let the big German in, then closed it behind them.

Grunewald looked around the room and then back to Noah Barrister.

"Not quite up to your usual standards, boss."

Noah smiled.

"It's temporary. We just have to finish this one task, and then we're done."

Noah could tell by the look on Grunewald's face that there was something about this idea that the man didn't like.

"What is it?" Noah probed. "Come on, out with it."

"This is what I do," Grunewald replied. "It's what we do. Me and the guys. The whole set-up at the hospital made it feel like we were part of a team again."

Noah finally understood. All he had been seeing was the finish line in front of him; his own resolution. He hadn't been looking at it from the perspective of the men. In a way, they were all once again about to be orphaned by the very state they had served for most of their lives. They would be tools without a purpose.

"So, tell me. What is it you want? If the choice were yours, which direction would you go in?" Noah asked.

Grunewald paused to think for a moment.

"To keep working, I guess. The rest of the guys feel the same. It's all we know. We don't really have families or friends outside of work. Hell, I guess work is our family. I also think there are a lot of important things we could do if we had the right leader."

Grunewald stared at Noah for a moment, and then the doctor understood. He was implying that Noah should be their leader.

"I... I'm not in this for the long haul," Noah said. "Not anymore."

"Why? What changed?"

"I've lost faith in the mission."

"Then we find another mission. Maybe we even make our own."

Noah thought about it. Perhaps Grunewald was on to something. It wasn't that Noah Barrister wanted to quit his work, and it wasn't really true that he had lost faith in the mission. No, he had just lost faith in the leaders.

"Okay. I'll find a new mission," Noah said, and then he noticed the bruises to the side of Grunewald's face. "Who in the hell managed to rough you up?"

"Some cow puncher who came with the group that busted out Bonafide," Grunewald said. "And when I find him, he's going to look a hell of a lot worse than I do right now."

"I think I might know where he went."

"Really?" Grunewald asked.

"They're CIA. I'd bet my last nickel on it. In which case, they'll have exfiltrated to a nearby safe-house. There are only three in the area, and I have the addresses."

"So, we hit them?"

"No," Noah said. "That's the wrong move. Deploy three of your men to sit on them. We run standard surveillance and look for a weakness we can exploit."

"What about me?"

"I do believe there's a former patient of ours waiting for a package. I want you to deliver it to him."

CIA Safehouse
Washington D.C.
March 20, 1981

"This is everything we have," Clark said, indicating the row of six syringes laid out on the card table.

"Six doses," Angela said thoughtfully. "That means he only has six tries to get this thing under control."

"And not have a stroke," Mac said. "Right?"

"Yes," Angela replied. "Just remember this wasn't my first choice."

"How long will it take?" Scarn asked.

"The effects of a dose of epinephrine usually wear off in ten to twenty minutes. But with how fast

Jack's heart is beating, it's probably going to be closer to ten. Maybe even less."

"He might have to do this for an *hour*?" Clark asked in disbelief.

"He can do it," Mac interjected. "He's made it through a lot worse."

Angela looked at Mac, and he could see the doubt in her eyes.

"He can do it," Mac insisted.

Angela nodded.

"Who's going to inject him?" she asked.

Mac and Clark both hesitated. Carrie stepped forward.

"I'll do it," she said.

She reached out her hand, and Scarn pressed the first syringe into it.

Jack was sitting in a wooden chair. Mac secured his arms to it with nylon straps and then secured his legs as well. He looked into his brother's eyes. He had never seen Jack like this before.

He looked like he was about to break in half.

"I can't stop the voices," Jack said quietly.

"I know, brother," Mac said. "I've been there. Just push through it."

Mac stood up and stepped away.

"So when should we—" Clark started, but he was

interrupted by Carrie jabbing the syringe into Jack and working the plunger.

Angela stood in front of Jack and gripped his arms as his eyes went wide and he clenched his teeth.

"*Breathe,*" Angela said calmly. "You have to breathe. Slow it down. Go to a different place. Escape the chaos."

Jack's breathing was fast, at least one inhale and exhale per second. The veins in his arms were bulging, and his skin flushed. Then he stopped breathing.

"Breathe!" Angela shouted, and she slapped him hard across the face.

Jack suddenly pulled in a slow breath, and his body seized.

"I'm sorry, Jack," Angela said. She turned to Carrie. "Hit him again."

"What?" Clark asked. "I thought we were supposed to wait ten minutes?"

"Do it, goddammit!" Angela shouted.

Carrie answered by snatching up a second syringe and slamming it into Jack's chest. His body surged again, and Angela gripped his arms harder. She could feel his pulse pounding. It was at least three hundred beats per minute.

"Breathe! Slow it down! Get it under control, Jack."

Jack Bonafide's body slammed back and forth against his restraints as the wooden chair began to splinter. Angela could feel her own body slick with cold sweat as her terror built. Was she about to kill this man?

Angela could feel that Jack's breathing was starting to stabilize, but it wasn't enough. She needed to push him harder. It was the only way, and she knew it. She turned to Carrie.

"Hit him again!"

It had been three minutes.

"What?" Carrie asked, her eyes wide.

Angela reached out and grabbed the third syringe.

"What are you doing?" Mac demanded.

"Saving his life!"

She plunged it into his leg and watched him surge again.

"If you don't get this under control right now, you're going to die!" Angela shouted. "Everyone you love will die!"

Jack arched his spine, drew in a deep breath, and then his body relaxed as the breath slowly rolled back out of him. The next breath was also slow, and the next, and the next.

He relaxed his body and looked at Angela.

"You came," he said.

Robard's Halfway House
Washington D.C.
March 20, 1981

Sid sat on the edge of the bed reading his copy of *1984*. Beside him lay the revolver, the hammer pulled back, ready to go. He looked down at his hospital slippers and then back to the book. He liked the slippers. They were comfortable. They reminded him of home.

There was a knock at the door.

Sid had left it unlocked, because if someone was stupid enough to come in without being invited, they would be in for a world of hurt.

The knob turned, and Sid picked up the .38.

"Whoa there, Kemosabe," Grunewald said, holding up his hands. "I come bearing gifts."

Sid smiled. Grunewald had always treated him

fairly, and he was the one who had told him about the mission God wanted him to undertake.

The mission to destroy the Thought Police.

Sid released the hammer on the .38 and returned it to the bed. He stood up and shook Grunewald's hand.

"I'm glad to see you," Sid said. "I've been a little lonely."

"Well, thought you might like a visitor," Grunewald said. "Are you taking your medication?"

"Yes," Sid said. He reached into his pocket and retrieved the prescription bottle. "Just like you told me to."

Grunewald knew something that Sid did not. The pills were the very thing making him crazy. Otherwise, he would be just one more PTSD case; probably no danger to himself or anyone else.

The pills changed that. The pills made him a weapon.

"Good," Grunewald replied. He handed Sid a folder. "I have something for you."

He handed Sid a folder. "It's the travel itinerary containing the location where they'll be meeting. I'll have your credentials soon, as well."

Sid opened the folder and pulled out the sheet of

papers. They detailed every known impending movement of the President of the United States.

"Soon," Sid said. "Soon."

"Do you have your faces ready?" Grunewald asked.

Sid nodded.

A CIA Safehouse
Washington D.C.
March 20, 1981

Jack sat on the edge of the cot drinking water. He had taken down nearly half a gallon. Angela had already done her due diligence, taking his vitals and checking for any lasting signs of trauma. While Jack seemed to be fine, she had suggested he get a full cardiac workup done as soon as possible to assess how much strain his heart had taken.

When they had started the procedure, she had known right away that it wasn't working; his reactions had told her that. Based on this quick assessment, she had done the only thing she could think of: she accelerated the timeline, counting on Jack's genetics and superior conditioning to get him through it.

Fortunately, it had worked. The contrast of adrenaline and breathing had snapped Jack out of his state of high anxiety. Privately, Angela had to admit to herself that success was a one-in-a-million shot. He should have died.

Scarn pulled up a chair and sat down across from Jack.

"Never thought I'd be glad to see you," Jack said with a smile.

"The feeling is mutual," Scarn replied. "I know you've been through a lot, Jack, but we need to empty out that head of yours. You said someone was going to kill the President?"

Jack took another pull from his water bottle and then nodded.

"When I was inside, there was this guy named Sid. He seemed to have a real problem with the President. Had photos of him with the eyes crossed out and everything."

"Okay, but there are probably a thousand other guys out there doing the same thing. What makes this Sid any different?"

"He was able to make a mask that made him look just like me."

"What?"

"He said he used to make them for Hollywood. I'm telling you, Scarn, this guy is some kind of genius artist or something. If he was standing more than a few feet away from you wearing this mask, you'd think it was me."

"Shit. That's a problem."

"But it doesn't have to be me," Jack said. "I mean, *he* doesn't have to be me. He could be anyone."

"Okay, that definitely seems actionable."

"And we need to look into Doctor Barrister," Jack said. "That guy isn't your run-of-the-mill psychiatrist."

"I know," Scarn said. "He's one of ours."

"*What?*" Jack asked incredulously. "He's CIA? What in the hell is going on?"

"Cool it. We didn't know you were there," Scarn reassured him. "In fact, we didn't even know the place was in operation. It was an undisclosed wet works shop."

"I know," Jack said. "He made me kill people."

Scarn sat back in his chair, visibly taken aback.

"*Jesus,*" he said. "I'm sorry, Jack."

"It wasn't anyone who didn't have it coming," Jack said. "But it should have been my choice to make."

"Understood."

"So, who the hell *is* Doctor Barrister?"

"He was one of the lead guys on MK Ultra," Scarn explained.

"Fantastic," Jack said sarcastically.

"After that project went down the tubes, it looks like they let him write his own ticket as long as it was black book, so he concocted this whole idea. It was supposed to be some kind of garbage disposal for enemy agents we couldn't prosecute but also didn't want to just ship back home."

"But, of course, that didn't go as planned."

"No," Scarn said. "We've got forensics on site right now turning it inside out, and it's looking more and more like he was doing some private contracting, sending other people down the garbage disposal for a fee."

"How in the hell does something like this happen?" Jack snapped.

"I wish I could answer that," Scarn said. "Tresham was the first Director in twenty years to open all of the sealed files. That means something. Things will change."

Jack wanted to keep pushing—he was angry and wanted someone to pay for what had happened to him—but, at the same time, he knew that wasn't productive.

"So, what do we do now?" Jack asked.

"We have to find this guy you're talking about. Tresham already has people out looking for Doctor Barrister and the orderlies. Looks like they were all ex-CIA contractors."

"I have a couple names. I doubt they ever thought I'd get out, so they probably weren't using pseudonyms."

"What were they?"

"One guy was named Grunewald. Big German guy."

This caught Mac's attention, who had been standing nearby and was listening to the exchange.

"I think I whipped his ass in the hallway."

"Other guy was named Foster," Jack said. "If we can find him, he might be able to help."

"Why do you say that?" Scarn asked.

"Something about him," Jack answered. "The others all liked their job a little too much, but Foster seemed like he was there out of a sense of duty."

Mac sat down across from Jack.

"What the hell happened to you?" Jack asked.

"I was dead," Mac said. "At least, for a while. They brought me back."

"Who? How?"

"Another CIA-supported group called the Coal Chamber. Run by a woman named Daniel Flynn. They used some old MK Ultra stuff to jumpstart my nervous system, or, at least, that's how she explained it."

"I'm glad as hell to see you, brother," Jack said.

Mac smiled.

"How did two Texas boys like us get tangled up in all of this?" he asked.

"Bonafide family luck," Jack said.

Mac thought about telling his brother that he had less than a year to live, but he thought better of it. News like that could wait for another time.

The Office of the Director
CIA Headquarters
Langley, Virginia
March 20, 1981

"This is a mess," Tresham muttered. He had been saying the same thing over and over again for the past few hours as he thumbed through the sealed files. "A real mess."

In his hands, he held the penultimate file, with the final one sitting on his desk beside him. The file he was going through detailed some particularly nasty back door dealings that had occurred during MK Ultra, which, if released, would send at least a few Senators and Congressmen to prison, most likely for the rest of their lives. Despite the seriousness of the crimes, Mike Tresham had already privately decided that he was going to hold onto these chips to cash in at a later date. Ordinarily, he didn't like doing that sort of thing, but he was becoming increasingly aware that, in his position, it was a necessity to have that kind of a debt in your back pocket.

He lay the file down and shook his head, then picked up the final one. He tore off the seal and dumped the contents onto his desk.

"You have *got* to be shitting me," he said, eyes wide as he read the cover page.

A CIA Safehouse
Washington D.C.

March 20, 1981

Former US Attorney General David Kelvin opened his eyes to see a motley crew standing before him. He remembered Carrie, Clark, Mac, and Scarn from his dealings with them before he passed out, but they were stood with some woman who looked like she should be teaching a yoga class. And, most surprisingly, included among them was Jack Bonafide.

He looked down at his hands and saw that he was tied to a chair. The last thing he remembered was sitting in the back of a car.

"What in the hell is going on here?" Kelvin thundered.

"Torture," Carrie said. She stepped forward, pulled a switchblade from her waistband, and clicked it open. "Or, at least, it will be soon, if you don't talk."

"How dare you?" Kelvin continued. "People will be looking for me!"

"No, they won't," Scarn said. "You see, no one seems to like you all that much. I should know, because people also don't like *me* very much. So, no, Mister Kelvin, no one is looking for you."

Kelvin glanced around the room as if looking for help and then slumped back in the chair.

"What do you want?"

"You said you knew something about Soviet spies," Carrie said.

"Well... I didn't think I would actually have to tell you," Kelvin said.

"Spill it!" Carrie demanded.

"I don't think so," Kelvin replied. He leaned back in the chair, and a sly smile crossed his face. "Yes. I don't think I'm going to tell you much of anything."

Carrie turned to the others.

"Get out," she said.

"What are you talking about?" Scarn asked.

"If you aren't here, you can't be held responsible."

Scarn looked to Jack, who nodded.

Jack, Scarn, Angela, and Mac walked out the door without a word. Clark hesitated for a moment, but then he followed the others.

Scarn closed the door and let out a breath. Night had fallen.

"What's she going to do?" Clark asked.

"I'm pretty sure she's going to torture him," Mac said. "I thought you were supposed to be smart."

"We can't just let her do that," Clark insisted. "Right, Scarn?"

Michael Scarn looked uncomfortable. He had been thrust into the role of a leader ahead of his time. It was true that this was something he had always wanted, but now that it was his reality, he found himself feeling ill-prepared.

Scarn looked up toward the second floor where they had left Carrie with Kelvin and then turned back to Clark.

"You know, it's the strangest thing," Scarn said. "When I came here, there was no one to be found. So, I guess I'll be heading back to Langley."

Clark's face fell. He had been counting on Michael Scarn to be the one to advocate what Clark thought was the right thing. It wasn't that Clark thought Kelvin was innocent, or that he didn't have information they needed. It was that Clark Finster still believed good guys wore white and bad guys wore black, and there were certain lines that just weren't crossed.

Torturing Americans on American soil was on that list.

Without another word, Scarn walked down the sidewalk toward his sedan.

"I like that guy better now," Mac said, "than the last time I saw him."

Jack walked away from the group to where Angela Merril stood on the corner. She seemed shaken.

"Are you okay?" Jack asked, putting a hand on her shoulder.

She turned to him, her eyes wide.

"I've never done anything like that before," she said. "I could have killed you."

"But you didn't."

"But I could have!"

Jack looked into her eyes until they softened. She put her hand on his chest.

"I never thought I'd see you again. After Bethesda, I thought that was it."

"Well, here I am," Jack said with a smile.

Angela looked up at the building and then back to Jack.

"I don't know if I can go back in there," Angela said. "She's torturing that man."

Jack wanted to say something to assuage her concerns, but he knew there was nothing to say. It was true. If Carrie had to torture Kelvin to get him to talk, then that was exactly what she would do. It was a million miles away from what Jack had thought he stood for just a year prior, but he also now realized there was no other way. Not if the threat they had uncovered against the President was credible.

He looked around the neighborhood. It seemed safe enough.

"We'll have to go back in soon," Jack said. "You can wait out here if you think you need to."

"Then what?" Angela asked.

"We'll get you home. It's the least we can do."

"Do I have to cut off one of your ears to make you understand that I'm serious?" Carrie asked.

"I do believe you will have to do just that," Kelvin said, still smiling. "Give it a rest, Miss Davidson! I know how the CIA works. I know what you people are capable of, but I also know you have your limits."

Carrie closed the knife and slid it into her pocket. She pulled a pack of cigarettes from her jacket pocket and shook one loose into her hand.

"Do the words 'Coal Chamber' mean anything to you?" Carrie asked.

Kelvin's breathing changed. His muscles tensed.

"Flynn sent you," he surmised.

"I sent myself," Carrie replied.

"I'm still not telling you shit."

There it was again: that same personality shift she had seen in the car.

Carrie nodded her understanding.

"Remember when you could get loosies at the corner store?" Carrie asked. She put the cigarette between her lips and lit it. "You know what loosies are, right?"

"Yes, I know what fucking loosies are!" Kelvin snapped. "What the hell does that have to do with anything?"

"It's germaine!" Carrie shouted.

Her behavior seemed to snap Kelvin out of his smirking attitude. He was beginning to realize that there was something wrong with this woman.

"When I was a girl, I had this friend, Brad. His dad would send us down to the corner store to get him a loosie, but just one. Just a single cigarette. Then we'd head back to his house, and that would be it. I'd go home." Carrie paused for a moment and took a drag off her cigarette. "The next time I would see Brad, he would have a burn mark on him. His dad would get the idea Brad had done something wrong, maybe taken some extra food or something like that. So, he'd make him get that single loosie. You know what the real bitch of it was, though? It wasn't getting burned with that cigarette that was the real punishment. It was the walk to the corner store. It was the waiting. It was the time ticking by, counting down until he was going to get burned.

"You might be thinking that I'm the dad in this equation," Carrie snarled. "But I'm not. I'm the fucking corner store, and I've got enough loosies to make you sing any tune I damn well please. So, start talking!"

"Fuck you!" Kelvin shouted back. "There's nothing you can do to me that will measure up to what they'll do if they find out I talked."

"We'll see about that."

With her left hand, Carrie took the cigarette from between her lips and pressed it into the back of Kelvin's right hand. The man screamed and strained against the straps holding him to the chair. Carrie responded by dipping into her jacket pocket with her right hand and returning with a pair of brass knuckles. Kelvin continued screaming until she slammed them into the side of his head.

Carrie stepped back and looked at him. He was out cold.

She put the cigarette between her lips and took another pull before reaching into her left pocket and retrieving some smelling salts. She broke the packet open beneath Kelvin's nose, and his head whipped back in surprise.

"All day long," Carrie said. She dropped the brass knuckles back into her pocket and then opened the switchblade again. "Still think I'm bluffing?"

"Tolya Rodin," Kelvin said quickly. "That's his name. *Tolya Rodin.*"

"We already knew that. It's in the logbook."

"Yes, but you don't know who he is. Who he *really* is."

This caught Carrie's attention, and Kelvin knew it.

"So, who is he?"

"I want immunity."

"We barely work for the government at this point. You're not getting immunity."

"Not from the government," Kelvin said. "From Flynn."

Carrie cocked her head to the side in obvious surprise.

"What is it between you and her? Why does she want you dead?"

"That doesn't matter," Kelvin said. "Not if you

want to know who Tolya Rodin is. Suffice to say she couldn't touch me when I was the Attorney General, but now that I'm not? It's open season. That's why you're here, after all, isn't it? To kill me?"

Carrie didn't answer. She just stared at Kelvin with a coldness he had experienced few times in his life.

Jack turned to the sound of the door opening and saw Carrie walk out onto the street. She looked different than when he had last seen her back in Upstate New York. She looked harder, more worn.

"Are his balls still attached?" Jack asked.

"For them to still be attached, they would have to have existed to begin with." Carrie paused for a moment and shook her head in obvious disgust. "We're going to have to deal with him. He knows who Tolya Rodin is."

"You think he's telling the truth?" Jack asked.

"Yeah, I do. He knows too much. He knows about Flynn—the woman we're working for—and he seems to be in the loop."

Jack thought about it for a moment and then nodded his understanding.

"What do we need to do?"

"Get him out of the country," Carrie said. "I've got some forgers I can tap for a new identity, and we can scrounge up some cash for him. The thing is, he's not worried about prosecution. He's running from Flynn."

"So, there's some bad blood there," Mac cut in.

"Going way back," Carrie confirmed. "But if you want to crack open this Tolya Rodin problem and stop the Executive Branch from falling through the proverbial basement, we have to make this work."

"Agreed," Jack said. He turned to Mac. "I hate to ask you to do this."

"Shit," Mac groused. "Then *don't*."

"I have a safehouse in Canada," Carrie said. "I made some contacts when I blew through Quebec on my way to Siberia. All you have to do is get him there and sit on him until we can arrange for something more permanent."

"I'm being benched," Mac surmised.

"You're *not* being benched," Jack insisted. "This is the most important part. Remember how sometimes you had to pass the ball to me so the team could have the touchdown?"

Mac didn't want to answer, because he knew his brother was right.

"This is one of those times," Jack went on. "If we

don't get that information from Kelvin, we can't get the goddamn touchdown. If they're going after the President, we have to stop that from happening. No matter what it takes."

"I get it," Mac said. "I don't like it, but I get it."

CHAPTER 5

CIA Headquarters
Langley, VA
March 20, 1981

MICHAEL SCARN WALKED QUICKLY across the polished floor of the outer office and was about to knock on the door to the office of the Director when Eleanor Babbitt swung it open and came face to face with him.

"Oh, good," she said. "Maybe he can yell at you for a few minutes. I need a break."

"What?" Scarn asked.

Eleanor didn't answer as she walked by him and made a beeline straight for the bank of elevators.

"Scarn!" Tresham shouted. "Get in here!"

"Shit," Scarn whispered under his breath.

He stepped into the office and closed the door behind him.

Tresham was standing at his desk, holding one of the formerly sealed envelopes.

"There's a fucking vial of *anthrax* in Los Angeles!"

"What are you talking about?" Scarn asked.

"Exactly what I said! We allowed a vial of anthrax to be shipped to L.A. three months ago to try and chase down whoever it was going to."

"That seems ill-advised."

"No shit, genius," Tresham stopped for a second and let out a long breath. "Sorry. You didn't deserve that."

"What are we looking at?" Scarn asked, ignoring the slight. "What's the op profile?"

"We have a small team in place that's been tracking this vial since it entered the Port of Los Angeles. They're sitting in a safehouse in North Hollywood right now. I already had the Ops Chief reach out and tell them to hold fast and that someone is coming out to them."

Tresham paused for a moment, and Scarn held his gaze.

"Ah," Scarn said. "I'm the someone."

"I need someone with firepower—specifically, rank—to handle this. I just need an on-the-ground assessment of what's going on and your opinion on whether we should pull the operation or not."

"I have a hard time seeing how this could be a good op."

"I agree, but it's closed loop. Only the team on the ground has the real dope on what's going on, so I need you to link up and find out just what the hell that is." Tresham scribbled some notes on a piece of paper and handed it across the desk to Scarn. "This is the address and the name of the team leader. Guy's name is Pritchard Jones."

Scarn looked at the paper for a moment.

"I know him," Scarn said.

"You do?"

"Yes. We went through The Farm together."

"What's your read on him?"

"He was a strange guy. Had this idea in his head that he wanted to be a NOC."

"That's never good," Tresham said and shook his head.

"Yeah, but he was solid otherwise. Just, you know, strange."

"Like you?" Tresham asked with a smile.

"Fuck you," Scarn laughed. "Hey, I think I've come a long way."

"You know, Scarn, I have to give it to you. Six months ago, if someone had told me you'd be Assistant Director, I'd have told them they should have their head examined. Now? Well, I'll just say you're right. You *have* come a long way. Now you have a long way to go. Specifically, to Los Angeles."

"Will do," Scarn said.

"Oh, wait," Tresham said. "What the hell happened with the whole hospital thing?"

Scarn stopped and seemed to think about it for a moment.

"You don't want to know."

"Goddammit!" Tresham shouted. "I could do without any more fucking sealed files."

"Trust me on this one," Scarn assured him. "It's under control. Jack and Carrie on it."

"Wait, what? You found Bonafide?"

"He was in Saint Elizabeth's. It's a long story, sir. They'll reach out directly when they have something actionable."

"Great. Just what I need. Jack Bonafide and

Carrie Davidson running around Washington D.C. unchecked."

"Clark's with them, if that makes you feel any better."

"No, Assistant Director, *that* does not make me feel any better."

A CIA Safehouse
Washington D.C.
March 20, 1981

David Kelvin sipped the cup of black coffee Clark had brought him and winced as he gripped the cup. The cigarette burn on his hand was on prominent display.

"I need medical attention," Kelvin said.

"Talk," Carrie replied.

"It could get infected," Kelvin countered, indicating the burn mark.

Carrie retrieved her brass knuckles from her jacket and glared at him.

"Jesus!" Kelvin shouted. "You know, you have some real anger issues. I think someone has been reading a little too much Gloria Steinem, if you know what I mean."

"Look," Jack said. "You're getting what you want, but the more time you spend screwing around, the more likely it is that we won't have time to put your information to use. My brother Mac here has orders that if the President dies, you're next."

Kelvin looked over to the younger Bonafide brother, who smiled.

"Won't be no thing but a chicken wing to me," Mac said. "So, I wouldn't push your luck."

"Fine," Kelvin said, looking around as if a Soviet spy was in the room somewhere.

"Tick tock," Jack said.

"Do you remember Richard Feldman?" Kelvin asked.

"Of course," Jack replied. "Arkady Radovich was sent to kill him but had a change of heart. Then you pardoned the son of a bitch."

"Didn't you ever wonder why Radovich came to kill him?"

"Some industrial espionage job," Jack said, although it was clear he was beginning to realize there was more to it than that.

"Try again," Kelvin said with a sneer. "Radovich came to kill a rogue KGB agent."

Jack's face fell.

"You can't be serious," he said.

"As a heart attack," Kelvin replied. "Richard Feldman is Tolya Rodin."

"*Son of a bitch!*" Jack snapped.

"More than that," Kelvin went on, "*I* was the one who got him into the United States all those years ago, back when I was a congressman. I established his new identity and set him up at a hedge fund in New York."

"Why in the hell would you do that?" Carrie demanded.

"I thought it would be an asset to have a former KGB agent with all of his connections in my back pocket," Kelvin said sheepishly. "Except it ended up being the other way around."

"Rodin played you," Jack said. "But you didn't dime him out because you would have gone down with him."

"And he never really asked for much. Some expedited paperwork here and there, but otherwise he was mainly quiet for years."

"Until?" Carrie asked.

"Until Radovich showed up. Then I get a call out of nowhere demanding citizenship and immunity for him. I tried to push back, but something had changed. It was like the KGB agent in him suddenly woke up from a long nap. Then the logbook surfaced. That was when Rodin really turned up the volume. Insisted I needed to track it down for him. That was why I came on so strong when Tresham was trying to find it."

"Because if you didn't, he would have let the world know who you really are," Jack surmised.

"Exactly. Not that it matters much anymore. I'm out of a fucking job."

Carrie drew her pistol and put it to Kelvin's head.

"Stop!" Jack ordered.

Carrie whipped her head toward him, the surprise obvious on her face.

"What?"

"You can't just kill him!" Jack demanded.

"Why not?"

"We've already done a lot of shit today I'd rather not have had to. I'm not adding cold-blooded murder to the list."

Carrie stared at Jack for a moment and then holstered her sidearm and sighed.

"Fine, Captain America. I won't shoot him," she said. "Just yet."

Kelvin let out a breath. He had been holding it

the entire time.

"At least someone still has some honor around here," Kelvin scoffed.

"Don't push it," Jack said, pointing a finger at Kelvin. "Your ass is still on thin ice."

Carrie turned to Mac and pushed a manila envelope into his hand.

"Cash, itinerary, and papers," Carrie said. "We shouldn't be more than seventy-two hours behind you."

"What then?" Mac asked.

Jack glared at Carrie.

"Fine, fine," Carrie said. "If his information holds and we can stop this thing, we'll honor the terms of his deal. We'll most likely re-route to South America, and he can start his new life as a *gringo*."

Jack walked across the room to the window and looked down at the street.

Angela was gone.

Jack opened the front door and emerged onto the sidewalk. A cold wind blew across his face.

"What is it?" Clark asked as he exited behind him.

"She was supposed to wait here," Jack said. He

looked at the single streetlight. "She was supposed to wait for us to give her a ride home."

"Maybe she caught a cab?" Clark asked.

Jack looked down at the street and saw a single tube of lipstick on the ground. He knelt down and picked it up. It was hers. He knew it.

"No. You didn't see the look in her eyes. She wouldn't have left alone."

"It was good that you didn't fight back," Grunewald said. "Too many people do, and it just turns into a big mess. The kind of mess that takes chemicals to clean up."

He looked at Angela Merril in the rearview mirror and then returned to the file folder he was going through. She was obviously terrified but had taken his warning to heart. She had gone quietly when they found her standing on the street corner.

McMichaels had done well sitting on the building and phoning in when he saw Bonafide comforting the woman. Then Jack had just left her there, ripe for the plucking.

Grunewald wasn't sure what they were going to do with her, but he remembered what Doctor Barrister had said. They might need some kind of leverage over Bonafide. A way to stop him if the usual methods proved not to be enough.

It was true that Jack Bonafide was a formidable operator; Grunewald had watched Jack kill several men with his own eyes. Back then, none of them had truly known who he was. He had been checked in as just another head case.

Now, the truth had come out. He was CIA. Not only that, but Bonafide was a founding member of the elite Delta Force. Grunewald privately wondered how he would measure up against a man like that himself. In their previous altercations, the big German had always been wielding a cattle prod. What if he didn't have that weapon? Could he go toe-to-toe with Jack Bonafide and walk away the victor?

"What are you going to do with me?" Angela asked.

"Nothing if you co-operate." Grunewald turned around in his seat. "I know it's hard to see this, considering our introduction and current circumstances, but we're the good guys."

"I'm having a really hard time with that idea," Angela replied.

Grunewald turned back around and faced the windshield.

"That's okay," he said. "Sometimes I do, too."

"I know what you're thinking," Carrie said. "But we can't go after her."

Jack set his jaw and then nodded.

"I get it."

Down the street, he noticed the car they had driven to the safehouse in was rocking.

"What in the hell?" Carrie asked.

"Shit," Mac said. "Yahtzee. We forgot him in the trunk."

Mac opened the trunk. Yahontov sprang out in an effort to attack but was quickly gripped by the much stronger Mac Bonafide and slammed into the pavement.

"Knock it off!" Mac shouted. "I still haven't decided if I want you alive yet!"

"Let him go," Jack said.

"What?" Mac asked.

"Trust me," Jack insisted.

Mac raised his hands and stood up from where he had dropped his knee into Yahontov's stomach.

The Russian stood up slowly and looked around

at the group.

"You won't last five minutes out there," Jack said. "The CIA took down the hospital and Doctor Barrister. They'll be looking for you. We're your only play."

"I'll be fine," Yahontov said in his thick Russian accent. "I've got out of tighter spots."

"Like in that hallway?" Jack asked. "Where I had to tourniquet your leg? Or maybe you mean in the hospital where I busted you out?"

Yahontov said nothing.

"All we need to know is who hired you for the job on CIA Headquarters," Jack said. "Then, you walk."

"I need more than that," Yahontov said. "If you really want me to turn that man over, I need extradition."

Jack turned to Carrie.

"Jesus Christ!" Carrie exclaimed. "What are we running here? A travel agency for villains?"

"Can you make it happen?" Jack asked.

Carrie glared at Jack for a moment and then shrugged.

"Where do you want to go?" she asked Yahontov.

"Somewhere warm. I don't really care. But I want a new identity and traveling money."

"Fine," Carrie said. "We can get you there."

Yahontov turned back to Jack.

"I don't know his name," he said. "I only saw him once."

"But if you saw him again, would you recognize him?" Jack asked.

"Of course."

Jack turned back to Clark.

"Do you have a dossier on Feldman?"

"Not to hand," Clark replied. "But I can pull something if we get back to my apartment."

An Undisclosed Location
Washington D.C.
March 20, 1981

Arkady Radovich finished jotting some notes down on a piece of paper and turned to Tolya Rodin.

"They're ready," he said.

Tolya leaned back on the leather couch and took another sip of his drink before answering the unasked question.

Arkady noticed that the man had changed.

When they had first met in Tolya's apartment in New York, the man had not been much to look at. He was pudgy and soft, his eyes wet and expectant. Now, his eyes were hard and knowing. Tolya had been exercising again and was steeling his body. He was returning to his roots, each day becoming more the former KGB agent and less the pampered American. As a result, Arkady now respected the man more than he had a month prior.

"What are your thoughts?" Tolya asked.

"They seem to be adapting to the changing environment. They still have their man poised to make an attempt on the President, but they are also setting up a blocking force."

"I expect that will suffice."

"You said you had a contingency," Arkady said.

"Yes."

Arkady waited, but Tolya did not continue.

"And?" Arkady asked. "What is it?"

"You," Tolya said.

"Ah," Arkady said. "I see."

"I am not throwing you to the wolves, my friend," Tolya assured him. "But I know who you are. I know the man you are. If these men fail—if their assassin fails—that means Jack Bonafide has once again derailed our best efforts."

"And you think that I am the man to end him," Arkady concluded.

"Who else could it be?" Tolya asked, shrugging.

"No one, I suppose," Arkady said. He reached across the bar and pulled a bottle of vodka toward him.

The Apartment of Clark Finster
Washington D.C.
March 20, 1981

Clark looked at his watch as he worked his key in the lock. It was nearly midnight, and he could feel it. He hadn't slept much the night before and imagined that he was functioning on only a few hours' sleep. Despite his tiredness, he worked hard to maintain a stoic demeanor. He wasn't hanging out with a bunch of analysts who were anxious to work on their Dungeons and Dragons characters. These were warriors, and even if he didn't feel like he was even close to their level, he at least needed to act the part.

The door swung open, and Clark flipped the

switch to turn the light on. Carrie was the first to enter the apartment. She looked around.

"Jesus," she said. "How many serial killers live here?"

"Why does everyone keep asking me that?" Clark exclaimed.

The rest of the group staggered in.

Jack slammed the door behind him.

"Okay, listen up!" Jack said. "We have a job to do and no time to do it in. Clark, pull a dossier on Feldman. Yahontov, confirm the identity, and then you're out of here. Carrie, get Mac prepped with anything else he needs to extradite these two assholes."

Clark had been busy digging though a pile of file folders on his desk, shortly returning with a single photo. He held it up to Yahontov.

"It's not him," Yahontov said.

"Shit!" Mac spat.

Clark held up a single finger, indicating that everyone should wait. He came back with another photo.

Yahontov tapped it with his index.

"That's him."

"I had to be sure," Clark said. "The first photo was Clint Eastwood."

"Who is Clint Eastwood?" Yahontov asked.

"He's like a worse version of me," Mac smiled.

Clark turned the photo around for everyone to see.

It was Feldman.

"Bingo," Jack said.

"So, what now?" Carrie asked.

"I'm gonna kill that son of a bitch," Jack said.

"You know I'd rather have you here with us," Jack said to his brother.

Mac stopped stuffing the duffel bag full of gear and turned to Jack.

"I know, and I get it. I get why it's important to get these guys out of the country." He paused for a moment. He wanted to tell Jack about what had happened to him and his diagnosis, but, once again, he decided that the time wasn't right. "I'll get them to Carrie's guy in Canada, and then we're off to South America."

"I'll see you on the other side," Jack said.

"Hate to interrupt," Carrie cut in, "but we've really got to get this show on the road. Clark pulled some intel on a local residence registered to Richard Feldman. Rodin has a house over in Maryland. We can be there in an hour."

Mac turned to where Kelvin and Yahontov were sitting on the couch.

"Okay, listen up, because I'm only going to say this once. I am your travel agent, and I do not take any shit." He pointed at Yahontov. "If anyone asks, you're my brother." He then pointed to Kelvin. "And you're my grandfather."

"Grandfather?" Kelvin spat. "How old do you think I am?"

"Refer back to the part about me not taking any shit, Grandpa," Mac said. "Now, let's go; we've got a train to catch."

Mac walked the two men out into the hallway and then turned back to where Carrie was standing inside the apartment. Something needed to be said.

"Can I have a word with you?" Mac asked.

Carrie looked confused but nodded and exited with him.

"You two," Mac said, indicating Kelvin and Yahontov, "wait downstairs. Don't get in trouble."

"Aren't you concerned we'll make a run for it?" Kelvin asked.

"I'm faster than you are," Mac said. "I'd shoot you down before you made it too far."

"Fair enough," Kelvin said with a nod.

Carrie stood in silence as the two men descended

the stairs to street level, leaving her alone with Mac in the hallway.

"What is it?" Carrie asked.

"We never talked about it," Mac said. "Not since Siberia, and now I'm not sure if there'll be another chance."

"About what?"

"About Falls Church. About what happened," Mac said and then corrected himself. "About what *would* have happened."

"Nothing happened," Carrie said. "Arkady's men saw to that."

"But it would have."

Carrie wasn't looking at Mac, and he picked up on it. She was looking through him.

"But it didn't," Carrie said. "I'm not saying I didn't feel something back there, but that was a different time. I was a different woman."

"You've changed that much?" Mac asked.

"You tell me, cowboy."

"You tortured that man."

"I came here to kill him," Carrie countered. "Seems to me he got off easy."

"I don't think 'Falls Church Carrie' would have done either," Mac said.

"There are a lot of things she wouldn't have

done," Carrie said coldly. "But she's gone and I'm here. And I get shit done."

Jack watched as Carrie re-entered the apartment and closed the door.

"It's the right thing to do," Clark said. He could sense that Jack was uneasy about the situation. "Honoring what we said we would do."

"Then why does it feel wrong?" Jack asked.

"The right thing usually does," Clark answered.

"Do you have that address?" Carrie asked him. "For Tolya Rodin?"

"Wait," Jack said, holding up a hand. "We've made this mistake before."

"What are you talking about?" Carrie asked.

"Going all in with no sleep."

"We're on a tight timeline."

"I get it," Jack said. "But stopping to grab a few hours' sleep will pay off. Trust me. I'm still trashed from all that shit flowing through my veins. When was the last time you slept?"

Carrie's eyes blinked rapidly.

"I don't know. It doesn't matter."

"Clark?" Jack asked.

"Few hours last night, but that's it."

Jack turned to Carrie.

"Am I running the show?" he asked.

Carrie clenched her jaw for a moment, but then she nodded.

"Then I need you to back the plays I make, and one of them is getting some sleep so we don't start making bad decisions."

Carrie was out within a minute, lying flat on the floor with her jacket over her face. Jack crashed on the couch while Clark tied off his robe.

"Why the robe?" Jack asked. "We'll only be asleep for a few hours."

"I'm an insomniac," Clark said. "The robe helps me sleep. It makes me feel safe."

Jack laid his Colt on his chest and pulled back the hammer.

"*This* makes me feel safe," he said.

Jack studied the young analyst for a moment.

"I know you never gave up looking for me," he said. "If it weren't for you, I'd probably still be in that place."

"You would have found a way out. Seems to me you were finding a way out when we got there."

"Maybe," Jack said. "Maybe not."

Clark sat down in the La-Z-Boy and kicked the footrest out.

"Something like that is hard to talk about," Clark said. "But to get past it, you might need to, at some point. To really put it behind you."

"You're probably right," Jack said. "I've just never been the talking sort."

"Well, if you ever need to... I'm around." Clark looked at Jack for a moment. "Are you seriously going to fall asleep with a cocked pistol lying on your chest?"

"Are you seriously going to sleep in that robe?"

"Takes all sorts, I guess," Clark replied.

Robard's Halfway House
Washington D.C.
March 20, 1981

Sid worked carefully on the latex with the scalpel Doctor Barrister had personally given him. Realizing he was holding his breath, he slowly exhaled. That was a bad habit that he needed to break. It was holding him back in the perfection of his craft. He knew that his brain didn't work as well when he stopped breathing.

Sid set the scalpel down on the scarred surface of the old wood dresser and looked again at the photo of the Secret Service agent he had taped to his mirror. He then looked to the mask and again returned to the photo.

Slowly and carefully, he applied the mask to his own face using the spirit gum, careful to remove any residue. He then went to work with the concealer, making sure the skin tone of his neck perfectly matched the skin tone of the mask.

It took a full twenty minutes to perfect the application, but Sid never became bored or frustrated with the process, no matter how long it took. It was his gift; a gift he knew was about to write him into the history books.

Sid straightened himself out and looked in the mirror, his own reflection cast beside that of the Secret Service agent in the photo.

He was Sid no longer. Staring back at him was Secret Service Agent Stephen Lister.

The Home of Stephen Lister
Washington D.C.

March 20, 1981

Stephen Lister looked at his kitchen table and frowned. How long was he going to keep doing this? How long would he continue to set a place at the table for a wife and daughter that had left him nearly a year prior?

Until they came back. That was the answer. He knew he needed to do more to make that happen, but with Regan in office now, his job had become even busier. The Secret Service really didn't care if you had a family or what that family thought about the hours you kept or the frequency of your travel. It only cared about one thing: protecting the President.

Ultimately, that was what had driven Stephen's wife away: her firm belief that he loved the President more than he did her. Of course, the idea was laughable.

Unlike most of his compatriots, Lister had actually thought very highly of President Carter and was not happy when the man was voted out of office. He didn't necessarily think there was anything wrong with Regan or his policies, but he also thought it was a bad idea to change horses mid-race, and that was exactly what America had done.

No, Stephen was not in love with the President. He was in love with the office. He was in love with what it stood for and, more importantly, what America represented. He saw himself as a sentinel standing at the gate, protecting something greater than himself.

He also knew that he was protecting something greater than his family. It made him both ashamed and proud to admit the fact to himself. It was an inner conflict that vexed him greatly. In Lister's mind, if the country fell apart, that meant his family would, as well, and so the country had to come first.

Stephen walked back to the stove and looked at the feast he had prepared. It was a feast for one.

The doorbell rang. Stephen looked up from the stove. It wasn't possible, was it? He had invited them over for dinner, but, as always, his wife had just answered with a stream of accusations and demands for more money. Had she had a change of heart?

Stephen smiled at the thought and walked across the kitchen, through the living room, and to the front door. He was about to open the door when he stopped himself. He was being foolish. Basic security protocols still needed to be observed. He tapped the pistol secured to his hip and leaned forward to look through the peephole.

Beyond was a woman. She looked to be in her late twenties. There was nothing threatening about her. In fact, she looked a little scared. It also didn't hurt that she was not unpleasant to look at.

Stephen opened the door.

"Can I help you?" he asked.

"I'm sorry," Angela Merril said quietly.

"Two fingers," Grunewald said as he stepped out of the darkness to the right of the door, his suppressed .22 pistol pointed at Stephen. "Out of the holster. Do it now."

Stephen complied. He was no coward, but he also knew when he was hopelessly outmatched. This man had outflanked him and was clearly serious.

"Don't do anything you'll regret," Stephen said as he pulled his pistol out with his thumb and index finger and handed it to Grunewald. "I'm a federal agent."

"I know," Grunewald said. "That's why we're here."

Angela Merril sat across the kitchen table from Stephen Lister. Stephen's right hand was handcuffed by a length of chain to the stove door. Grunewald stood at the same stove, finishing the cooking that Stephen had started.

"Not many people know how to cook a chicken properly," Grunewald said. He turned to Stephen and smiled. "But you were on your way. Just a little too much seasoning. You know what they say, don't you?"

It was clear that Grunewald wanted some kind of an answer.

"No, I don't," Stephen said.

"It takes a tough man to make a tender chicken."

"Look, I know why you're here," Stephen said.

"Oh, do you now?" Grunewald asked.

"I'm on the Presidential detail," Stephen said. "It doesn't take a rocket scientist to do the math."

"We're not going to kill you, if that's what you're worried about," Grunewald said. He looked to where his compatriot, McMichaels, was standing in the living room. "We're just like you. We're patriots."

Stephen studied the man at the stove for a moment and then nodded his head.

"You *are* just like me, aren't you? You're government."

Grunewald turned back to the chicken, although Stephen could see that he had caught him off guard.

"What makes you think that?" Grunewald asked.

"There's just something about you. We all have it. It's hard to quantify."

"That it is," Grunewald said. "You may be more right than you know."

"Is this some kind of training exercise?"

Grunewald laughed.

"No. Unfortunately, it is not."

Grunewald reached down and clicked off the burner. He shifted the frying pan to another part of the stovetop and reached for the salt. He turned around.

"This doesn't have to end badly," Grunewald said. "I mean, how much of a villain can I be? I just cooked you what will probably be the best chicken you will ever taste. I will be leaving soon, but my friend here will stay with you. Think of him as your minder."

"Then what?"

"Then... nothing. Sometime tomorrow, you will be released. No muss, no fuss."

"But we've seen your face," Stephen said, taking a calculated risk.

"I don't exist," Grunewald said with a shrug. "Not in any government or Interpol database."

Grunewald walked to Stephen and looked down

at him.

"Are these really questions you want to be asking?" he inquired.

Stephen locked eyes with the man for a moment, but he understood the implied threat.

"I guess not."

"Good," Grunewald said with a smile.

Stephen took note of the smile. He knew what a fake smile looked like, and he'd seen enough smiles that were meant to be menacing. This was neither of those. This man was being legitimately friendly toward him. If nothing else, Stephen knew that the man honestly believed they were on the same side.

Grunewald returned to the stove, plated the chicken, and then set one dish down on the table in front of Stephen and one in front of Angela. He stood there expectantly, beaming from ear to ear.

Stephen and Angela looked at each other, and Grunewald picked up on their hesitation.

"Well, it's not poisoned," Grunewald declared, "in case that's what you're thinking. If I wanted you dead, I would have just shot you, wouldn't I? I wouldn't ruin a perfectly good chicken to do it."

Stephen seemed to consider it for a moment and then went to work slicing off a piece of the chicken. He put it in his mouth and chewed it thoughtfully for a moment before swallowing. Angela watched him intently, obviously waiting for him to begin foaming at the mouth.

"Shit, that's good," Stephen said.

"See?" Grunewald asked. "Everything will be fine. I have some work to do, but you will be left in the very capable hands of my compatriot."

Grunewald headed for the door and then stopped and snapped his fingers. He turned around and faced Stephen.

"I almost forgot," he said. "Your credentials. I need them."

"My credentials?" Stephen asked, then understood. "My Secret Service credentials."

"No, your Ovaltine decoder pin. Little Orphan Annie is in trouble." Grunewald waited for a moment and then realized that the reference was lost on the much younger man. "Yes, Agent Lister. I need your Secret Service credentials."

"They're at work," Stephen said, without missing a beat. "I left them in my work jacket."

Grunewald walked across the room and stopped beside Angela.

"That's too bad," he said as he pulled his gun from its holster and put it to Angela's head. "Then she will have died for nothing."

"Wait!" Stephen shouted. "The table in the entryway. They're in the left drawer."

"Go along to get along, Agent Lister," Grunewald said, holstering his weapon. "This doesn't have to be hard unless you make it that way."

Grunewald walked back to the kitchen counter and looked at the wine rack mounted beside the sink. He tapped the cork of each bottle until he settled on one and pulled it out. He looked around for a moment and then turned to Stephen.

"Corkscrew?" Grunewald asked.

"Top left drawer," Stephen replied.

"You like that top left drawer, don't you?" Grunewald commented with a smile.

He retrieved the corkscrew and went to work on the bottle.

"I know about you," Grunewald said. "I did my homework. So, please don't be offended if I say this is a pretty nice vintage. In fact, it's so nice that it's out of character."

"It's my wife's," Stephen said. "Ex-wife's."

"Will she be cross with me?" Grunewald asked. "For opening it, I mean."

"Fuck her," Stephen said.

Grunewald laughed and poured three glasses.

"My friend is in AA," Grunewald said,

nodding toward the living room where McMichaels sat. "So, don't think me rude for not offering."

"Isn't that supposed to be anonymous?"

"I've been known to break a rule or two," Grunewald said with a wink.

Grunewald set one glass down in front of Stephen and another in front of Angela.

"Raise your glasses," Grunewald said. They both complied. "And let's have a toast."

"To what?" Stephen asked.

"Not doing anything stupid enough that it gets you killed."

Train Station
Washington D.C.
March 20, 1981

Mac Bonafide looked up at the departure boards and found the information for the sleeping car he had booked to take them to Canada. It was a bit of an extravagance, but he figured he had earned it for getting stuck with babysitting duty.

"What in the hell is in Quebec?" Kelvin grumbled.

"Nothing," Mac said. "That's the point. Trust me, I would have much preferred Montreal. Pretty girls."

"You've clearly never been to Montreal," Kelvin sneered.

"Is Quebec warm?" Yahontov asked.

Mac turned to Yahontov and raised an eyebrow.

"Yeah, it's like Hawaii," Kelvin laughed.

"Hawaii?" Yahontov asked.

"Oh," Mac said. "You're one of those guys."

"What guys?" Yahontov asked.

"Top guy in your unit, killed a hundred men in Afghanistan but don't know how much a loaf of bread costs?"

"Or what Hawaii is," Kelvin added.

Yahontov thought on this for a moment.

"So... Quebec is warm?"

"Yeah," Mac said. "You're that guy."

David Kelvin looked to the bank of pay phones on the wall before returning his attention back to Mac Bonafide. He knew he needed to make the call soon, but he had no idea how in the hell he was going to get it past the younger Bonafide brother.

CHAPTER 6

The Apartment of Clark Finster
Washington D.C.
March 21, 1981

CARRIE OPENED her eyes to the beeping of the phone stashed in her duffel bag.

She looked over and saw Clark hunched over his computer in a bathrobe and Jack passed out on the couch. For a moment, she thought about everything Jack had been through. It was a miracle he was still alive. Without him, there was no way they'd be able to pull this off. He was the type of man who was the lynchpin that kept an operation going; that kept a team like this together.

She sat up and rubbed her eyes, then indulged in letting her thoughts run wild for a moment longer. What they were doing was important. Not only was it important, but it was something that could decide the future of America. It could be the difference between them continuing to move toward the dream her father had fought for during World War Two or living in the nightmare of George Orwell's *1984*. They were only a few years shy of the latter, so the idea wasn't that far-fetched.

Another thought came to her. It was one she had already suppressed several times before. What they were doing was of crucial importance, but ultimately, she didn't care. All of this was happening because the American people had long ago lost the understanding of their own freedom, the very freedom that was so essential to their survival.

Was it possible that something else needed to happen to reinvigorate the resolve of the American people and unite them in the same way her father's generation had rallied against Hitler and Tojo? Something between the so-called "American Dream" and *1984*?

The beeping continued, and Clark eventually looked over his shoulder.

"Are you going to get that?" he asked.

"Yeah, yeah, yeah," Carrie said.

She stood up and dipped her hand into the over-stuffed bag, retrieving the phone. She hit the button to take the call and placed it to her ear.

"What in the hell is going on?"

It was Daniel Flynn. Carrie winced. She remembered that she was supposed to have given a situation report at midnight.

"Flynn," Carrie said. "Sorry. I forgot to check in."

"Is Kelvin dead?"

"No," Carrie replied. "The situation has evolved."

"Which seems unlikely," Daniel replied, "given that there is only one moving part. A bullet coming out of the back of David Kelvin's head. Are you telling me that hasn't happened?"

"He had intel relating to an impending threat on the President's life."

"I don't give a shit!" Flynn snapped. "Kelvin is the job! Not the President!"

Carrie was taken aback. Flynn's reaction didn't make any sense.

"I made a safe assumption that a viable threat against the President of the United States would supersede whatever personal vendetta you have against a disgraced Attorney General."

There was silence on the line.

"Personal vendetta?" Flynn asked, mild disgust in her voice. "Is that what you think this is?"

"If not, then what is it about?" Carrie countered.

"Fifty million dollars in Nazi gold financing the biggest massacre in American history," Flynn said curtly. Whatever Carrie had been expecting, it wasn't that. "Oh, did that get your attention?"

"I didn't know."

"That's why we follow orders, Carrie! Where the hell is Kelvin now?"

"On a train to Quebec."

"Jesus Christ!" Daniel spat. "Who with?"

"Mac and some Russian we busted out of Saint Elizabeth's."

"You need to get ahold of Mac and tell him to execute Kelvin," Daniel said. "Because the moment he gets to a phone and initiates that transfer, it'll all be over."

"What's going to happen?"

"An anthrax attack that I've been trying to stop

for the past six months. The puzzle was almost complete, except for one last piece."

"Kelvin had to die," Carrie surmised.

"That's right. But you fucked that up."

"I don't understand. How could he be involved in something like that? He just seems—"

"Pathetic?" Flynn asked. "Only a danger to himself? You only saw the version of him that he wanted you to see. There are two David Kelvins."

The line went dead.

"Shit," Carrie said quietly.

Jack sat up on the couch and looked at her.

"What's going on?" Jack asked.

Carrie looked ashen.

"I think I really fucked up."

Jack and Clark listened to Carrie relay the whole story of her assignment from Flynn, and how she and Mac had elected to go in a different direction.

"Okay," Jack said. "We're going to have to handle these things one at a time. Clark, send word of the attack up the chain to Scarn. They can get someone on it if it's actionable."

"*If* it's actionable?" Carrie asked. "Jack, I'm telling you this woman is for real. If she's saying

Kelvin somehow had a hand in getting anthrax into this country, it's really happening."

"I get it," Jack said. "But we can only do what we can do. We know the threat to the President is real, and we're already knee-deep trying to stop it. We have to stay the course and pass the ball on the anthrax threat to someone else. There are multiple agencies set up to handle something of that scale."

"Mac's with him," Clark said. "If Kelvin really is some kind of evil mastermind, he's probably in danger. Is there any way to get in contact with Mac? Warn him?"

"No," Carrie said. "We had him go dark specifically to avoid anyone tracking him, and that includes us."

"He'll be fine," Jack said.

"How can you know that?" Clark asked.

"Because he's a Bonafide," Jack said. "And it'll take more than David Kelvin to put an end to him." Jack stood up and crossed the room to Clark's intel board. "Now, where are we at?"

It was clear that Clark wanted to pursue the matter of Mac being on a train with a possible psychopath, but he took his cue from Jack and returned to the task at hand.

"I pulled a roster of all the patients at Saint Elizabeth's and cross-checked it against the list generated for when the Agency hit it. There are a few patients missing. Looks like you were right. One of them is named Sid Felton."

"Background?" Jack asked.

"Vietnam veteran, former Army airborne. Graduate of Hamburger Hill."

"Shit," Jack said. "No wonder that guy looked like he had a screw loose."

"It gets better," Clark said. "After that, he went to work for Hollywood and developed some new skills. Bet you can't guess what they were."

"Special effects?" Jack asked.

"That's right. His speciality was masks, and they were so good that unless you were right up to him, you couldn't tell the difference."

"Just like you said," Carrie said to Jack.

"There's more," Clark said. "Three years ago, he vanished."

"What do you mean?" Jack asked.

"I mean he fucking vanished. No bank accounts, no passport renewal, no taxes, no nothing."

Carrie and Jack looked at each other.

"Please don't tell me he went to work for us," Carrie said.

Clark threw up his hands.

"There's no paper trail that prove it, but it's too much of a coincidence that three years after this guy drops off the face of the earth, he shows up in a CIA black site half out of his mind and intending to kill the President."

"So where do we find him?" Jack asked.

"If Barrister is running this whole thing, he's too smart to sock him away in a known safehouse, but it would still have to be a place he knows is secure."

"A daisy chain," Carrie said, referring to a contract series of linked safehouses that would be impossible to trace, usually set up by non-official cover operatives.

"Probably," Clark replied. "My guess is we're looking for some kind of a halfway house. Probably as low-rent as you can get."

"Any possibles?" Jack asked.

Clark reached back to his desk and handed Jack a sheet of paper.

"Six on the list. They're all close enough to the hospital and dodgy enough to be likely, but it's still really grasping at straws."

Jack looked at his watch and saw that it was two in the morning.

"If we're going to hit them, this is the perfect time," Jack said.

"Unless Felton doesn't sleep," Clark said.

Jack handed the sheet to Carrie.

"Again?" Carrie asked, taking it from him.

"Ours is not to question why," Jack said with a smile.

"There's something else," Clark said, and he grabbed a Post-it note from the wall. He passed it to Jack. "This address came across the police band while you were asleep."

"What is it?"

Clark shook his head.

"Nothing, I'm sure, but it still seemed strange. A woman called in a police report on her husband. He's a Secret Service agent, so I thought it might be relevant."

"What did he do?" Carrie asked.

"It's what he *didn't* do. She said he always calls her around midnight, begging her to come home. Sometimes he's half in the bag, and sometimes he's sober."

"So?" Jack asked.

"Last night, he didn't call."

"Still," Jack said. "Isn't that a bit much to call the police over?"

"He's done it every night like clockwork for the past year."

Jack looked at the address and then back to Clark.

"Okay," Jack said. "I'm going to run this down." He turned to Carrie. "Feel better?"

"Immensely," she smiled.

"What about you?" Jack turned to Clark.

"I feel pretty good," Clark replied.

"No, Clark. I mean what are you going to work on while we're running down these leads?"

"Oh." Clark sat back down at his desk. He tapped a few keys on his computer, and the screen changed. "I've been running down financial records for everyone involved in this, particularly Doctor Barrister."

"And what did you find?"

"Nothing," Clark said. "That's the problem."

"What do you mean?"

"Well, it's pretty obvious Barrister tried to cover his tracks, but he actually did too good a job of it. Everything is *too* perfect. So, I'm following the trail and eventually it should take me to—"

"Tolya Rodin," Jack finished for him.

"Yes. We already know about the Richard Feldman identity, but he'll definitely have other accounts, shell corporations, et cetera." Clark turned and looked at Jack. "I know you want to take this guy down yourself, but we have a lot of plates spinning right now. If I get all of this information and just forward it to the Bureau, they can do the takedown."

Jack set his jaw. Clark was right. He wanted to be the one to put that son of a bitch on his face and let him know that his days of being the puppet master were over. The fact of the matter was that Feldman had played him for a fool, and that left a bad taste in his mouth that he'd like to get rid of.

"Okay," Jack said. "You're right. Get what you can, and then send a package to the FBI. Go directly to Agent Fields."

"Got it."

The Stardust Diner
Washington D.C.
March 21, 1981

Sid Felton sat alone in his booth at the Stardust Diner, but he wore the face of Stephen Lister.

He had quite enjoyed the pancakes he ordered, but he'd washed them down with a cup of admittedly sub-standard black coffee. However, to Sid, it was worth noting that even sub-standard black coffee was still black coffee, and it got the job done.

Overall, Sid had to admit he felt good. In fact, he felt good for the first time in quite a while, and it wasn't just the lithium. Ever since Central America, he had felt off. That was how he had ended up in Saint Elizabeth's. The mission he'd been given just didn't feel right. It didn't speak to his soul.

Then Doctor Barrister had changed all of that when he taught Sid about the Thought Police and what they wanted to do to the children of America. There was no way Sid could just stand idly by and allow something like that to happen, not after how hard he had fought in Vietnam to protect those same Americans from the spread of Communism.

Not only was he now going to stop the spread of Communism, but he was going to stamp it out for good.

The bells on the front door jingled, and Sid turned to see Grunewald enter.

"I can't stay long," Grunewald said as he slid into the booth and passed an envelope beneath the table to Sid. "Here's what you need."

Sid took the envelope and opened it, still keeping it beneath the table and out of sight. It contained the credentials he required to verify that he was, in fact, the man whose face he was wearing.

"Thank you," Sid said.

"You should know, they're onto you."

"Who?" Sid asked.

"The CIA. My guess is Bonafide has recovered by now and is at least involved in the effort. He knows what you look like."

"Kind of," Sid said with a smile.

Grunewald allowed himself to laugh.

"True enough. Just remember that you can't get caught. This meeting is so secret that even the CIA aren't aware of it. Just a handful of Secret Service agents and the Secretary of State are the only Americans in the know. No one can find out who you really are. They have to think you're Lister. They have to think Stephen Lister did this."

Sid nodded.

"I know. I've got it all mapped out in here," he said, pointing to his head. "Even if they are after me, they probably think I'm trying to kill the President."

"That was the point of all your crazy talk about Reagan drawing flies."

"Right," Sid said. "They don't know my actual target is the Soviet Premier."

The Home of Stephen Lister
Washington D.C.
March 21, 1981

Stephen Lister looked at the clock on the wall. It had been two hours since the man he assumed was the leader of the two had left. Their "babysitter" had remained in the living room, watching television and not saying a word to them.

While Stephen had been cuffed to the oven door, Angela remained free.

Stephen leaned forward.

"We have to do something," he said, and then corrected himself. "I need *you* to do something."

A look of panic quickly overtook Angela's face.

"Me?" she asked quietly, glancing at the man in the living room to see if he could hear them.

"I can't," Stephen said, indicating his restraints. "If I could, I would, but I can't. You can."

"What do you want me to do?" Angela asked.

Stephen nodded to the knife block on the countertop just a few feet behind her.

"If you can get that knife in him, even just a flesh wound, I'll have a fighting chance.

"Are you insane?" Angela blurted. "Earlier this afternoon, I was teaching a yoga class, and now you want me to—what? Stab a man?"

"Think of it like... I don't know, Primal Scream therapy but with a knife."

"You're out of your mind."

"Listen to me!" Stephen snapped. "In an hour's time, the President is going to be getting prepped for a secret meeting with the Premier of the Soviet Union."

"What?" Angela asked in disbelief. "Here?"

"Yes! They need to sort out what happened with the KGB last month, and they decided that it needed to be in person so they could look each other in the eye and read each other's souls, or some other bullshit. Brezhnev is in Washington to meet with Reagan, and these guys decide to pick tonight of all nights to sideline me and take my credentials?

"If I don't get out of this chair and sound the alarm, these guys are going to have direct access to the leaders of the United States and the Soviet Union in one shot!"

Angela nodded her understanding.

"What do you need me to do?"

Stephen leaned forward and lowered his voice.

"We need to get him in here, then I'll distract

him. Once he's entirely focused on me, you need to grab that knife out of the block and put it in him."

"I can't," Angela said, shaking her head. She was obviously terrified. "I just can't."

"You can!" Stephen hissed. "You *have* to!"

Angela froze for a moment, looking almost catatonic, and then nodded her head.

"Okay," she said. "I can do it."

"Can you get him in here?" Stephen asked.

Angela turned to look at McMichaels and saw him staring at her legs.

"It won't be hard," she said.

Robard's Halfway House
Washington D.C.
March 21, 1981

Carrie pushed open the front door of the halfway house and was pleased to find exactly what she was expecting. Specifically, it was a real shit hole. Ops always ran better when things made sense. The world felt—if only for a moment—as if it were spinning smoothly on its axis.

At the end of the small lobby sat what appeared to be a long-struggling man in his late sixties, working on what was probably his twentieth cigarette of the night, judging by his nicotine-stained fingers and teeth. He looked up from his newspaper and smiled.

Carrie knew that smile.

"Don't get any ideas, Gramps," she said. "It's not that kind of visit."

She pulled out the fake FBI credentials she had stashed for just such an occasion and flashed them to the old man.

"I run a clean house," he said, holding up both hands.

"Just as well I'm not arresting you."

Carrie pulled the photo of Sid Felton from her jacket pocket and placed it on the counter.

"I'm looking for this man," she said.

"Never seen him," the attendant replied.

"You didn't even look at the picture."

"Don't need to," he said, smiling through his nicotine-stained teeth. "Haven't see him."

Carrie had half a mind to just pistol-whip the man until he told her what she wanted to know, but instead she opted for finesse.

Carrie dug back into her pocket and smoothed a hundred-dollar bill out on the counter.

"He might have been with a man by the name of Benjamin Franklin."

"Don't you think it's odd?" the man asked.

"What is?" Carrie asked, taking the bait.

"Benjamin Franklin was never an American President, yet he's on the currency."

"I guess it is," Carrie replied. "But it's not exactly at the top of my list of concerns."

"Someone should look into it," Nicotine Man said as he leaned back and retrieved a key for Room Twenty-Four. He handed it to Carrie.

"Do you know if he's in?" Carrie asked.

Nicotine Man shook his head.

"I only look up from this newspaper for pretty girls."

Carrie walked down the dimly lit hallway and stopped in front of Room Twenty-Four. The place was a little livelier than she had expected for three in the morning. Radios could be heard playing in other rooms, and she could hear the distinct sound of a pistol being assembled. None of it was coming from room twenty-four, so she paid it no mind.

Nothing stood out about the exterior of the room, but she also had no idea if Sid Felton was in the building, so she decided to behave as if he was.

Carrie slipped the key into the door's lock while drawing her Beretta 1951 from the holster. She waited a moment longer, straining to detect any noise coming from inside. There was nothing.

With a quarter turn of the key, the lock disengaged with an audible *click*.

This was it. No more time for subtlety.

Carrie pushed the door open and brought her weapon up. Her movements were smooth and practiced. She quickly moved out of the doorway and cleared the corners. Within seconds, she knew she was alone. Sid Felton was not there.

Down the hall, she could already hear doors opening. Whenever you upset the equilibrium in a place like this, the residents somehow seemed to know. It also didn't help that most career criminals had a sort of sixth sense when it came to law enforcement. They could smell a cop a mile away, and it was a sure bet that Carrie Davidson was giving off quite a scent.

It was time to grab whatever intelligence she could and get the hell out of there. She was kicking herself for not having brought some kind of bag, but she saw a discarded garbage sack in the corner and grabbed that. Within a few minutes, she had stuffed several items into it and knotted it shut.

She was headed for the door when a business card stuck to the mirror on the wall caught her eye.

Carrie stopped and scanned it.

The Hotel Monaco

Carrie knew the place. It was one of the oldest hotels in Washington D.C. She snatched the card from the mirror and stuffed it in her pocket. She turned and saw a man standing in the doorway. A thick scar ran across the left side of his jaw. There was no expression on his face, and no emotion behind his eyes.

To his rear, Carrie could see Nicotine Man and a few others.

"That's her," Nicotine Man said with a knowing nod. He then turned and headed back for the stairs.

Carrie stood motionless and stared at the man in the doorway.

He said nothing.

She returned the favor.

"You're a real hardcase, ain't you?" he asked.

"Never had any complaints," Carrie said coldly.

He stepped forward into the room, and the other men followed. The last man in closed the door.

Carrie smiled.

"What's your name?" Carrie asked the lead man.

"Why?"

"So I know what to engrave on your fucking headstone if you don't get the hell out of my way."

The lead man laughed, a deep rolling laugh that went on for several seconds before he finally stopped. His reaction was reasonable enough, considering that he probably outweighed Carrie by at least a hundred pounds.

"You got a fucking mouth on you," he said. "We're just the Neighborhood Watch, honey, so why don't you tell me—"

Carrie drew her pistol, and the man froze. She then dropped the magazine to the floor and ejected the round from the chamber into her hand and pocketed it. She disassembled the Beretta and tossed the pieces on the bed.

The lead man's face changed.

"Why in the hell would you do something like that?" he asked, his confusion obvious.

"Because I'm bored and a little pissed," she said. "And you four look like a lot of fun."

Carrie was fast; much faster than she looked. She snatched an old lamp up from the bedside table and hurled it past the lead man into one of his followers. The lamp crashed against his head and knocked him to the floor, blood readily flowing from his split flesh.

Another turned toward the door and tried to open it, realizing that bad things were about to happen in a confined space. Carrie launched off her rear foot, moving past the lead man to grab the fleeing man by the back of his long hair. She used his own momentum to slam his face against the door and knock him out cold.

The lead man drew a pistol, and Carrie stepped into his arm, turning one hundred and eighty degrees to put her back to him. She grabbed his gun hand and yanked on it as he fired, forcing the round into the belly of the last follower.

She then bit down hard on his wrist, forcing him to drop the weapon.

Carrie stepped back and fired her right heel into the inside of the lead man's left knee, breaking it with a sickening *snap* that echoed off the walls. She knew it was the sound of his ACL popping. He fell to the floor and gripped the injured limb as he howled in pain.

Carrie threw a hard kick to his hands and

knocked them out of the way. She then stepped forward and ground her boot heel into his broken knee.

She looked down at him and smiled.

"I ain't no one's honey," Carrie said, her Tennessee twang standing out in bold relief. "And I've got no patience for rude men."

Finally, she released his knee, took a step back, and scooped his pistol up from the floor. She turned and fired three rounds, killing the three other men in the room. She dropped the magazine, ejected the round, and tossed the gun to the lead man. He reflexively caught it in a fumbling grip.

"That's murder one," she said. Carrie gathered up her things, including her disassembled pistol, and opened the door. "Enjoy your prison time, asshole."

The Quebec Express
New York
March 21, 1981

Mac Bonafide strained to keep his eyes open. He was not completely certain, but he estimated that he had been awake for nearly forty-eight hours. This stretch of wakefulness took him back to his time in the Teams and even reminded him a bit of BUDs, although he wasn't freezing his ass off this time.

Yahontov had passed out the moment they reached the sleeping car. Strangely, Mac liked the big Russian. He knew that, on paper, they should be mortal enemies, but Mac sensed that they were more alike than not.

Kelvin, on the other hand, was a different story. He just struck Mac as a little bitch. Mac knew that wasn't the politically correct thing to say, but he just couldn't come up with any other way to describe the former US Attorney General.

When they had arrived at the sleeping car, Kelvin had immediately begun complaining about the accommodation, insisting that he needed a larger bed to "stretch his legs out." After Mac had threatened to help him get some sleep by knocking him out, Kelvin had quietened down. Now, the man was off in the washroom doing God only knew what.

David Kelvin splashed some water on his face and looked at himself in the mirror.

He knew what he needed to do, but there was

just no way to do it. He looked down at his watch and saw that it was three in the morning. The East Germans were supposed to launch in nine hours, but if the money wasn't in the requisite account by the time they checked, nothing would happen.

Despite all the advantages his haul of Nazi gold had purchased him, Kelvin sometimes wished he had never met Heinrich Weber. Yes, the old Nazi had, in a way, made Kelvin the man he was today, but at what cost? What had he sold to purchase that future self? How had he become intertwined with Nazis and KGB agents?

The truth of it was, this was his way back in. It was his way back into the White House. He had always been the "law and order" Attorney General, and Kelvin knew damn well they still hadn't found someone plausible to replace him.

If there were some sort of emergency, some sort of disaster, they would have no choice but to call him back in. So, when Heinrich Weber had approached him and requested inside help with a small attack on a strategic American military facility, Kelvin had laughed in his face, which had taken the old Nazi aback.

"A shooting on a military base?" Kelvin had

mocked. "What if I help you up the ante by financing the greatest attack in American history?"

Once something like that happened, his phone would be ringing off the hook. There would be no time to select a replacement, no time for on-the-job training. They would be begging David Kelvin to return to the fold.

There was also Tolya Rodin's offer of the Governorship of New York. That wasn't a bad safety net to have in his back pocket, and so he had decided to play along.

David Kelvin looked at himself in the mirror.

"Maybe I shouldn't make the call," he said to his own reflection. "Maybe I should just settle in for the ride and start over again somewhere else. Somewhere warm. Or just let this governor idea play out with Tolya."

Dave Kelvin looked back from the mirror and narrowed his eyes.

"The hell you will," Dave Kelvin replied. "We've come too far for you to turn chickenshit now."

"It's not that," David said. "I'm just tired."

"Well, I'm not," Dave said. "So let me out."

David Kelvin stood up straight and stared at his reflection.

"No."

"Yes!" Dave snapped. "Just like we always have when there's some dirty work to be done and you're too much of a little bitch to do it. Let me out, and I'll find a way to make the call."

"No," David said and shook his head. "I can do it. Just give me a chance."

"I don't think so," Dave replied. He reached into the sink, ran some water across his hands, and then slicked his hair back. "I'm taking charge of this clusterfuck. Just like I did when I struck that deal with Weber and made the call to recruit Rodin."

Dave Kelvin stepped out of the washroom and back into the hallway of the rail car. He clicked the door shut behind him and checked his surroundings. It was quiet, just as it should have been for that time of the morning.

He thought back and realized it had been several years since he was last out, since he was the dominant personality within the man known as David Kelvin. He went by "Dave" to make things psychologically more palatable for the fragile David Kelvin, but the truth was that he was something else. Something more than just a man. He was just one of several fractured psyches within this shell. They were all pieces of the same puzzle. *He* was that puzzle.

Dave walked down the hallway until he reached the door to the shared sleeping car. He paused for a moment and listened. There was nothing. He clicked the door open and peered inside. The big Russian was asleep, out cold. Mac Bonafide sat on the edge of the lower bunk, staring out the window at the countryside flying by.

Mac looked over his shoulder.

"Took long enough," he said before turning back to the window.

"Yeah," Dave said. "Well, you know how it is. Had a lot of cord to unwind."

Mac chuckled. He watched the countryside rolling by in the night and then felt a strange sensation in the back of his brain. What the hell was it?

Something was wrong.

He started to turn, and then his body locked up. He reached back, but his attacker turned him and slammed his body against the bunk. It was Kelvin. He had him in a rear naked chokehold. Mac struggled but had no leverage.

He could feel the lights going out.

Dave Kelvin pushed Mac to the floor and sunk his hooks in as he clamped down on the rear naked choke. Mac Bonafide was physically much stronger than Dave, but the older man had the advantage of the element of surprise.

When he was locked away, Dave only ever did mental practice of moves like this. He just ran the same mental exercises over, and over, and over again. He did this because he knew his weaker half was just that; weak. Dave Kelvin had to be strong. He had to be able to impose his will upon men like him if he wanted to bring his plans to fruition.

Dave glanced over his shoulder and could see that Yahontov was still sawing logs. The big Russian had not even budged.

Dave felt Mac go limp in his grip. He waited another moment more and then released him. He quickly rolled Mac Bonafide over, opened his jacket, and removed the man's pistol. He decided to take the holster as well, securing it in his waistband beneath his suit jacket.

He moved quietly and grabbed a pillow from the top bunk. He looked down at Yahontov.

"Sorry," he said. "Can't risk it."

In one fluid motion, Dave Kelvin pushed the pillow against the Russian's head, then pressed the pistol into it and pulled the trigger. A cloud of feathers erupted from the pillow.

Yahontov was dead.

It had not been quiet. Yes, the pillow had muffled the report of the weapon, but the kill was by no means silent. Dave looked down and saw that Mac was already beginning to stir. He pointed the pistol at him and pulled back the hammer.

Something stopped him. Dave thought about it for a moment and then made the weapon safe again. He realized what had stayed his hand.

He liked Mac Bonafide. The man was a lot like him.

The Western Inn
Washington D.C.
March 21, 1981

Doctor Noah Barrister paced in circles around the small motel room. Everything was happening so fast. He felt like he just needed a few minutes to sit down and wrap his head around what was going on in order for him to feel more confident in his control of the situation.

It seemed that he had—almost accidentally—

become the leader of the group Grunewald had established. Before he'd had chance to take a breath, they were acting on behalf of Tolya Rodin, attempting to assassinate the Soviet Premier on American soil.

Noah stopped and thought about the ramifications for a moment. An event like that would shake the American democracy to its very roots. No, an event like that would shake the *entire world*. A man who could make something like that happen... well, a man of that capability could most certainly command whatever fee he wanted for a repeat performance.

Noah smiled at the thought. Perhaps this was the path he had been looking for; the mission he needed.

The phone rang. Noah reached out, picked up the receiver, and put it to his ear. He said nothing. This was the protocol they had established in order to avoid accidentally giving themselves away.

"We have a problem," the voice on the other end of the line said.

It was Gregerson, the man who had been managing counterintelligence for him at Saint Elizabeth's. Noah had no idea where Gregerson was now, as they had decided that this new organization would work remotely via a series of interconnected cells.

That way, if one of them was captured, it would not compromise the rest of the group.

"What is it?" Noah asked.

"Someone has accessed our accounts."

"Which ones?" Noah asked.

"*All* of them."

Noah paused for a moment. This was bad. Granted, he dealt mostly in cash and had gone to great pains to keep his financial records clean, but no one was perfect. A good enough investigator would always uncover something.

"Who is it?"

"An analyst from Langley named Clark Finster. He went into Special Projects a couple of months ago and has been dark since then."

"Do you think he's with Bonafide? Can he link us to Tolya Rodin?"

"I don't know," Gregerson replied. "But if it were up to me, I wouldn't just let him keep going down the path he's on. I think he's just doing a lot of guess-work right now, but if he keeps guessing long enough, eventually he'll guess right."

"I agree," Noah said. "Dispatch Pryor and Vega to his location."

"How should they approach him?"

"Interrogation," Noah said. "And then disposal."

CHAPTER 7

The Home of Stephen Lister
Washington D.C.
March 21, 1981

"WE HAVE TO DO THIS NOW," Stephen said, checking again to make sure their babysitter couldn't hear him. "You're nervous, I get it, but time is running out. The meeting is supposed to start soon."

"Okay, okay," Angela said. She leaned toward the living room. "Excuse me?"

McMichaels turned to her.

"What?"

Her voice was quavering slightly. "I need to... um, you know."

"What?" McMichaels asked again, obviously confused.

"I need to tinkle."

"Tinkle?" Stephen mocked.

"Shut up!" Angela snapped and then turned back to McMichaels. "It's kind of urgent."

"Fine," McMichaels said.

He stood up and crossed the room to the kitchen, careful to stay outside of Stephen's striking distance. He had been warned that this man was not someone to drop your guard around.

McMichaels stopped and stood over Angela expectantly.

"Well?"

"What?" she replied.

"Let's go."

"You're going with me?"

"I'm not letting you wander around on your own," McMichaels said. "So, let's go."

"Fine," Angela replied. She stood up from the chair and smoothed her skirt down.

She turned to where the knives were kept. A shot of cold fear raced up her spine. This was it. It was time.

McMichaels turned to lead her to the bathroom, and the moment his back was to her, Angela reached out and snatched a butcher's knife from the block. She moved as fast as she could, swinging it in a high overhand arc toward the man's back.

McMichaels was faster than she was. He spun around and grabbed her wrist with one hand, then snatched the knife with the other. He threw the knife away and came down with a hard overhand right that struck Angela in the face and knocked her to the floor.

She could taste blood in her mouth, and her vision was blurred. She pushed herself up until her back was to the kitchen counter. McMichaels stood over her, and then he hit the floor. In the confusion, he had gotten a little too close to Stephen, who had thrown a hard kick into his back.

It wasn't enough.

McMichaels turned around, snatched a pan off the stove, and slammed it against Stephen's head. The Secret Service agent wasn't out, but he was clearly dazed. Angela stumbled to her feet and braced herself against the counter. Then she felt it: McMichaels pushing himself up against her and grabbing the back of her head by her hair.

"Grunewald thinks he's some kind of fucking

Boy Scout!" McMichaels snarled. "But I'm not. And he didn't say anything about you needing to be alive when he came back. But we're going to have a little fun first."

"Trust me," Angela said, reaching out and closing her fist around the corkscrew Grunewald had left on the counter. "This won't be fun for anyone."

McMichaels spun her around, and Angela threw the same hard overhand swing she had attempted with the butcher's knife.

This time, she found her mark. She shoved the corkscrew directly into McMichaels' right eye.

Screaming violently, he stumbled back against the wall, reached into his jacket, and drew his weapon.

Fueled by a sudden surge of adrenaline, Stephen Lister grabbed the handle of the oven door he was chained to and yanked on it hard three times until the entire door came loose.

"No!" he shouted, turning and slamming the door into McMichaels' head.

The glass front of the oven door shattered as McMichaels' head smashed through it, jagged shards slashing his throat and spraying blood from his carotid artery across the room.

McMichaels dropped to a knee and then collapsed to the floor.

Stephen didn't pause to savor his victory, opting instead to search the pockets of their quickly dying captor until he retrieved the key to his handcuffs and was able to unlock himself. He was pulling the gun from McMichaels' trembling hand when he heard the sound of retching behind him.

Angela Merril was on her knees, vomiting. Stephen moved quickly to her and put a hand on her back.

"It's okay," he said. "This is normal. You just helped kill a man."

Angela braced herself against the cool tile of the kitchen floor and waited for the last of her stomach's contents to empty. She sat up and looked at Stephen, tears in her eyes.

"We have to move," Stephen said.

Angela nodded.

She stumbled to her feet, and Stephen took her hand.

"We're going to get out of here, get to the nearest phone, and call this in," he said. "We can't do it here; we have no idea when that maniac will be back, and I need to get you to safety."

"Okay," Angela said quietly.

Stephen crossed the living room with Angela behind him, the pistol held at his side. He stopped and checked the entryway table. Sure enough, his credentials were gone. What in the hell was going on here? What use were his credentials without him?

"Stay close to me," Stephen said as he reached out and opened the door.

Grunewald pulled the trigger of his suppressed .22 pistol, and Secret Service Agent Stephen Lister dropped to the floor, dead, a single, neat hole newly formed on his forehead.

Angela let out a bloodcurdling scream.

Grunewald turned his pistol on her and put a finger to his lips.

Angela stopped screaming.

"I thought I was pretty clear about not doing anything stupid?" her captor said.

The Apartment of Clark Finster
Washington D.C.
March 21, 1981

Clark pushed his glasses up over his forehead and rubbed his eyes. He had briefly thought about grabbing a quick nap, but then decided against it. He should have taken advantage of the time Jack and Carrie had been asleep to get some shut-eye himself, but the things he had been working on were just too compelling.

Now, that work was finally starting to bear fruit. While the Central Intelligence Agency was obviously not going to hold easily accessible information regarding Noah Barrister and his Saint Elizabeth's wet works project in any formal system, the money to fund it still had to come from somewhere, and Clark was quickly figuring out just where that "somewhere" was.

Specifically, a string of current and former CIA employees who had a history of doing work that others might find distasteful, and who had been on the receiving end of multiple disciplinary reports. After finding backdoors into their personal accounts, Clark discovered that they were all being paid quite well by a series of shell corporations.

All of this research had culminated in a list of names that Clark believed all worked for this shadow organization. The only real question remaining was how deep this all went, and who exactly was the head of the snake.

So far, all signs pointed to Tolya Rodin/Richard Feldman somehow being involved. All Clark needed was the figurative or literal smoking gun to sic the FBI on him, just like he had promised Jack he would.

Clark continued to scan through the numbers on his screen until he heard the creak of a floorboard being stepped on in the hallway outside his apartment. His breath caught in his throat. There was no way it was Jack or Carrie, because neither of them would be trying to stay silent as they approached his door.

Clark looked over his shoulder at the door as he slid his desk drawer open and reached for the nine-millimeter pistol within.

Vega kicked the door in and already had his weapon up, Pryor directly behind him.

"Don't be a hero!" Vega said quickly as he moved across the room.

Clark stopped and raised his hands.

"You're Rodin's men, aren't you?"

Pryor pulled Clark out of his chair, slammed him against the wall, and zip-tied his hands behind his back.

Vega looked the young man over and then pulled Clark's pistol out of the drawer.

"I'm guessing you're one of those guys who's too smart for his own good?" Vega asked.

"I get that a lot."

Vega reached back into the desk drawer and retrieved Clark's CIA credentials.

"Well, Mister Clark Finster," he said. "It's a real tragedy that you were so distraught over the abduction of your good friend Jack Bonafide that you took your life with your service pistol."

The Home of Stephen Lister
Washington D.C.
March 21, 1981

Jack shut the door of the sedan and looked around.

It was a quiet enough neighborhood, and a nice enough one, as well. It was the sort of place a man could raise a family. He thought about that for a moment, and, once again, memories of Angeline crept in from the darkness within. He pushed them away. It wasn't the time, but that response did beg the question: *when* would it be the time? When would he mourn her? What would that even feel like?

As it had turned out, he hadn't needed to mourn Mac, because his brother was still alive. Jack wasn't even certain he had fully processed that reality yet. The whole thing was unbelievable.

He looked at the address on the house he had parked beside and estimated that the home of Stephen Lister would be about a block further down. It was a long shot that this police call had anything at all to do with the supposed attempt on the President's life, but thinner leads than this had paid off recently.

Despite having been thrust into his leadership role, Jack still craved the life of the singleton. He'd done some missions on his own with Delta. In fact, he was the designated singleton within the Unit when it was called for. Yes, Jack was hell on wheels when it came to leading an assault team, but he could also be counted on to go off on his own and come back with another notch on his belt.

Jack tapped the Colt 1911 on his hip with his right hand and then the folding knife clipped into his hip pocket with his left. He could feel the weight of the .38 strapped to his right ankle and the Fairbairn-

Sykes fighting knife in its sheath pressing against his lower back.

He stopped at the foot of the driveway and looked around. It was quiet. He looked down at his watch. It was just shy of three thirty in the morning. The lights in the house were on.

That was wrong.

Jack walked down the street and then cut through the backyard of the neighboring house. He moved carefully through the yard in case there was a dog, but fortunately, there wasn't. He thought back to when Mac had stolen that dog in Virginia while they had been hunting the Directorate S agent Steven Waller, and he had a silent laugh about that.

He continued his wide loop until he landed in the backyard of Stephen Lister's house. He could see movement inside. Jack walked in a low crouch until he was right up on the slider. And then his eyes grew wide.

Angela Merril was inside. There was blood on her face. It was obvious that there had been some kind of a fight, and at the other end of the house, by the front door, he could see a body face down on the floor.

There was a man standing beside Angela holding what looked like a suppressed .22 pistol, but his face was obscured. Jack didn't know who in the hell this guy was, but he knew that he was in his way.

Jack reached down to his belt, unclipped one of the two flashbang grenades he had secured there, and walked quickly toward the slider. There was no time for finesse. It was time for violence of action.

Jack cocked his arm back and then slammed it forward, rocketing the grenade through the slider window, where it detonated with an incredibly loud noise and a harsh flash of light.

The former Delta soldier was right behind it, running through the broken slider and into the kitchen with his pistol ready. Grunewald tried to pivot and bring his weapon up toward the source of the attack, but Jack was faster than he was. He pistol-whipped him in the face with his Colt.

Grunewald fell to the floor but still tried to get his gun up, even despite the blood in his eyes.

"Stop!" Jack shouted, moving aggressively toward Grunewald with his weapon and stomping his foot hard on the floor. He needed this man alive. Now that he knew who it was, Jack worked hard to suppress the urge to give him a world class ass whipping.

Grunewald froze. As he blinked his eyes to clear

away the blood, he realized that it was Jack Bonafide standing over him.

Angela winced as Jack cleaned the small cut on her forehead from where McMichaels had hit her.

"This will need stitches," Jack said. He applied a small Band-Aid and then pushed her hair out of her face. "Are you okay?"

Angela shook her head. She looked over to where MicMichaels' body still lay on the floor, his head protruding from the frame of the oven door and the corkscrew lodged in his eye.

"I killed him," she said quietly.

"No," Jack replied. "The stove killed him."

He smiled, and she couldn't help her laughter, albeit terrified and nervous.

"Can you sit tight for a minute while I talk to this man?"

Angela nodded.

Jack stood up from where he had been kneeling on the kitchen tile and walked back into the living room. Grunewald sat on the floor, handcuffed to a heavy bookcase. Jack looked to the entryway where Stephen Lister's body lay face down on the floor. He had thrown a blanket over him, but it was already soaked through with blood.

"Who do you work for?" Jack demanded.

Grunewald cocked his head to the side quizzically.

"That's a strange question."

"How so?" Jack asked.

"Well... we work for the same people."

"The CIA?"

"It sure ain't the Girl Scouts," Grunewald said with a laugh. "Which is too bad. Their cookies are great. But only once a year. You want to talk about insidious plans?"

"Knock it off!" Jack shouted. "What are you talking about, you work for the CIA?"

"Come on, Jack! Think about it. You know we were running a clandestine wet works shop at Saint Elizabeth's. Hell, you were a part of it. We just didn't know who you were. If we had, we would have turned up the volume big time. Is it that big a leap to believe we're all Central Intelligence employees?"

"Then why the hell are you trying to kill the President?"

Now, Grunewald was truly surprised, and Jack could see it.

"Kill the President?" Grunewald asked. "Where in the hell did you get that idea?"

"Doesn't take a genius to work out what you were prepping Sid Felton for."

Grunewald smiled and nodded.

"You're good. After we figured out who you were, they told me you were good and they were right," Grunewald said, before suddenly becoming more serious. "But you're not *that* good. We're not trying to kill the President, Jack. We're *going to kill* the Soviet Premier."

"Brezhnev?"

"The very same. It doesn't really matter if you know at this point; there's no time to stop it. Reagan's almost there, Jack; he's almost in the zone. He's primed to step up to the plate and put the Soviet Union on notice. We're just going to help him along the way."

Jack looked to the dead body of Stephen Lister and then remembered Sid Felton's special talent.

"By making it look like one of the President's own killed Brezhnev," Jack said.

"There you go! See? I knew you were good. I *knew* it."

"You're out of your fucking mind," Jack said quietly.

"No, Jack, we're not crazy. In fact, we're the sanest of all in this entire equation. Doctor Barrister is a visionary."

"He's not acting alone, is he?"

Grunewald fell silent.

"Who's funding him? Is it Tolya Rodin?"

"Who the hell is Tolya Rodin?" Grunewald asked, and Jack could tell that he really didn't know.

"It doesn't matter anyway," Jack said as he headed for the phone. "I'm calling it in, and it'll be over with."

"I don't think so, Jack," Grunewald called out, looking to the clock on the wall. "The President's detail went dark thirty minutes ago. No comms in, no comms out."

"What?"

"It's true. The only people who even know this meeting is taking place aside from Reagan and the Soviets are the Secretary of State and the assigned Secret Service. Try if you want, but you won't get anywhere."

Jack picked up the phone and dialed the number for Clark's apartment. He waited while it rang.

"And I wouldn't bother calling Clark Finster," Grunewald said. "He is what we sometimes refer to as 'indisposed.'"

Jack felt cold. He turned to face Grunewald and set the phone down.

"What did you do?" Jack asked.

"Loose ends, Jack. Clark has a real talent for running down money trails. A talent like that can't be left unchecked."

Jack moved quickly toward Grunewald and put the muzzle of his Colt 1911 to the man's temple.

"Talk, or you die!"

"Let's play a game, Jack!" Grunewald shouted. "The Soviet Premier is about to be executed in the grand ballroom of the Hotel Monaco. Your little friend Clark is about to meet the same fate in his apartment. Who lives, Jack? Who dies?"

"Call it off!" Jack thundered, pressing the muzzle hard into Grunewald's flesh. "Do it!"

"I don't think so. You can kill me if you want, Jack, but it won't change a thing."

Jack stepped back and withdrew his weapon.

"You son of a bitch."

The Hotel Monaco
Washington D.C.
March 21, 1981

Eldred Parks stood in the alleyway behind the Hotel Monaco and squinted to see his watch in the darkness. He knew he should get one of those new digital watches you could read in the dark, but the old World War Two veteran was in no hurry to jump on board the train of progress that seemed to be pushing the entire world into the future far faster than he might like.

Eldred had been head of the Presidential protection detail for three months, and he had witnessed firsthand that progression toward the future. In fact, he was a part of it now in a very big way. One could even say that he had a front row seat.

Personally, Eldred thought the meeting was a bad idea. It had "disaster" written all over it. Just three Secret Service agents assigned to protect the President during what could prove to be one of the most crucial meetings in the country's history?

The door to the hotel creaked open, and Agent Wilkins stepped out into the alleyway. He was a good man. A little younger and less experienced than Eldred might have liked, but he was as solid as they came and had an eye for detail.

"All clear?" Eldred asked.

"Looks to be," Wilkins said with a nod.

Eldred looked to the end of the alleyway where the small sedan was parked. In it sat the President of the United States.

"I'd like to lodge my formal protest one more time that this is a bad idea," Wilkins said.

"Noted," Eldred replied.

That was all he could say. He couldn't tell the much more junior Agent Wilkins that he whole-heartedly agreed with the man's assessment, and that, in his opinion, this whole meeting was a dumpster fire waiting to happen.

Down the street, Carrie stood across from the rear entrance to the Hotel Monaco and checked her watch. She had tried to call the tip into Clark, but there had been no answer. It figured that this would be the moment the analyst would decide to take a nap.

She looked at a payphone down the street before focusing back on the entrance. She wondered if she should try to call it in again.

Then she noticed the sedan. It had been parked at the mouth of the alleyway for the entire time she had been there.

She pressed her fingers to her right temple. Her head had been throbbing for the past hour, at least. She looked back to the mouth of the alleyway.

There was no move to make, and so she stepped back into the shadows and waited.

Arkady Radovich sat in the darkness of the sedan and watched the lone woman monitoring the entrance to the Hotel Monaco. While he could not quite make out her distinct features, he knew that it was Carrie Davidson.

He reached over to the stack of file folders in the passenger seat and retrieved the one bearing her name. It was a personnel file marked with the seal of the Central Intelligence Agency. Arkady knew of Carrie Davidson, but he had never actually met her. The CIA's own internal documents speculated that she had gone rogue and was potentially in the employ of a foreign power. Much less official rumblings from within that same agency suggested she was, in fact, still within the the employ of the CIA as part of a black operations unit.

Arkady wondered how the CIA managed to survive with so much confusion and internal strife. Even Doctor Barrister's team had sprung from within the CIA and was now embroiled in a plot to assassinate the Soviet Premier.

He flipped through Carrie's file and then looked back to where she stood. The fact that she was here was not good. That meant someone had left a clue she had been able to pick up, and it had lead her straight to the Hotel Monaco. Tolya had been right to send him.

Arkady picked up the Motorola radio on the dashboard, and it chirped to life.

He thumbed the call button.

"Rattler, this is Bear."

He waited a moment until the call came back.

"This is Rattler. Send it."

"Ready the assault force. We may have a problem."

Eldred Parks looked at his watch and then back to the sedan.

"Where in the hell is he?" he snapped.

"This isn't like him," Wilkins replied. "I've known Stephen for years, and he's never been late. *Never.*"

Eldred could see there was something on Wilkins' mind.

"What is it?" Eldred asked.

"His wife," Wilkins said. "It's been bad lately. I mean, real bad."

"Bad enough to cause him not to show up for duty?" Eldred pushed.

Wilkins thought about it for a moment.

"Shit, I don't know—"

"I'm here!" a voice said from the street, followed by a figure jogging toward them.

"It's about goddamn time!" Eldred snapped.

Stephen Lister stopped and coughed into his hand.

"Are you sick?" Eldred asked.

"Came down with a cold or something. That's why I was late," Stephen Lister/Sid Felton said, taking a step back.

"Perfect," Eldred groused. "Stick to perimeter security. The last thing we need is you infecting the rest of the detail."

"Don't worry," Sid Felton said from behind his perfect Stephen Lister mask. "I'll keep my distance."

Carrie looked back to the payphone and sighed. She couldn't just wait there forever, and she knew it. She pulled a pack of cigarettes from her pocket and slapped it against her hand. She looked at the package and thought about the contribution they would make to shortening her life. Perhaps that was a good thing.

This was pointless, and she knew it. She had nothing else to go on aside from the name of the hotel, and if this attempt on the President was going to kick off, it would be soon. She didn't have time to wait around and hope a clue would land in her lap.

This was to say nothing of the supposed Anthrax attack Flynn had been so worked up about. Carrie sure hoped Clark was passing that further up the chain. If the threat was real, the shit was well and truly about to hit the fan.

Arkady Radovich watched Carrie walk from her position to her car. He then turned to the sound of a panel van pulling up beside his own vehicle.

"Should we go after her?" a man asked as he leaned out the window.

"No," Arkady replied.

"What do you care?" another man shot back.

Arkady stepped forward and glared at him.

"Do you want to die tonight?" he asked.

The operative relaxed the tension in his jaw and said nothing.

"I asked you a question," Arkady pushed.

"No," the man replied.

"Excellent," Arkady said. "Then let's focus on the job at hand. Are your men prepped?"

The rear doors of the van opened, and a man stepped out, a H&K MP5 submachine gun slung across his chest.

"We're ready," he said, before pausing for a moment, seeming as if something was on his mind.

"What is it?" Arkady asked.

"I don't know you," the man replied. "I was told you are now mission commander on the ground, but I don't know you."

Arkady was ready to hammer this man, but decided instead to dial his aggression down. He knew that he would react the same way if he were in this man's shoes.

"What is your name?" Arkady asked.

"Richardson."

"Richardson, my name is Arkady. I am an independent contractor," Arkady said. "My employer has retained the services of Doctor Barrister and, by proxy, your men. My employer does not doubt your skill or resolve, but he is understandably nervous considering the stakes that are at play. Because of this, he has asked me to oversee operations for the time being."

Richardson nodded his acceptance.

"So, what's the play?" he asked.

Arkady looked at his watch.

"Our man on the inside has thirty minutes to accomplish his task. If he fails, we will assault the hotel with overwhelming force and kill everyone in our path."

The Quebec Express
Canada
March 21, 1981

The train rolled to a slow stop at the station, and before it had even ceased moving, Dave Kelvin had already hopped off onto the platform. He would take care of some business and then find a car.

He had left Mac Bonafide trussed up like a prize pig in the sleeping car, so he had little concern that the man would sound the alarm and rat him out.

Dave thought about it for a moment. Why in the

hell hadn't he killed him? It was almost as if there were some link between them, something that was impossible to quantify but had stopped him from taking the younger Bonafide brother's life.

The train platform was shrouded in darkness, but Dave soon spotted the bank of pay phones near the small parking lot. He walked quickly to them, checking his watch along the way.

Dave snatched up a receiver and entered a long string of numbers. He waited as the customary greeting was given.

"Account number one-five-six-three-seven-eight-nine," Dave said. "Authorization code Bravo-Mike-seven-zero-niner."

"Are you quite certain, sir?" the representative on the other end of the line asked. "Once this amount of money is transferred, it cannot be recalled."

"Oh, I'm quite certain," Kelvin said with a smile. "This has been a *long* time coming."

CHAPTER 8

The Apartment of Clark Finster
Washington D.C.
March 21, 1981

CLARK BLINKED AWAY the blood in his eyes and tried to ignore the taste of it in his mouth. He tried to push it out of his mind so he wouldn't start panicking. That was the last thing he needed now. He knew that if he didn't stay calm, he was dead.

Vega stood over Clark and eyed him warily. Pryor was behind him, cleaning blood off his hands. Clark recognized there was a lot of it, and all of it was *his*.

"You're really not going to talk, are you?" Vega asked.

"I can sing and dance... if that makes you feel better," Clark replied.

He knew these men weren't buying his tough guy routine, but if he was going to die there in his apartment, tied to a chair, he sure as hell wasn't going to give them the satisfaction of seeing him turn into a sniveling coward. He also wasn't going to give up Jack and Carrie.

Vega smiled.

"You're not giving up," he said. "I respect that. I respect that a lot."

"Does that mean we can... call it even and... part as friends?" Clark asked, struggling to get the words out as his own blood ran down the back of his throat.

"I don't think so," Vega replied. "You got close, though. If that makes you feel any better."

"How close?" Clark asked.

"Just a couple of keystrokes away," Vega said. He turned to look at Clark's screen and nodded. "Not that it would have mattered much."

"Why not?"

Vega looked unsure for a moment and then shrugged.

"The man who secured our services wouldn't

have been home anyway. Do you really think he'd be sitting in his recliner at his house on the hill?" Vega shook his head. "No. A man like that; he's in a bunker somewhere. We don't even know who he is."

"Do you... understand what they're trying to do?" Clark demanded. "They're going to kill the President!"

"The *President*?" Vega laughed. "Is that what you think? We're not going to kill the President."

Clark was confused, and there was no hiding it.

"Then what are you trying to do?"

"We're going to force him to do the right thing."

The Hotel Monaco
Washington D.C.
March 21, 1981

Jack pulled his car up to the curb across from the Hotel Monaco and killed the engine. There were only a handful of streetlights on that early in the morning, but that could prove to be an advantage. The last thing he needed was a bunch of employees asking him questions.

"What are we doing here?" Angela asked.

Jack pulled out his Colt 1911 and did a quick brass check, then re-holstered it.

"I'm stopping this insanity before it starts," he said.

Jack opened the glovebox and pulled out a small pistol. He pushed it into Angela's hands.

"What in the hell is this?" she asked.

"It's a .38 Special. Do you know how to use it?"

"I'm a respiratory therapist!" Angela nearly shouted. "Why in the hell would I know how to use *this*?"

"I thought you might be from Texas," Jack said, looking back out the window. "They would have taught you in grade school."

"Ha ha," Angela said. "I'm glad you're getting a kick out of this."

"Can you pull the trigger or not?" Jack demanded. "I can't leave you here if you're not safe."

"I can do it," Angela said. "I'm just not happy about it."

"Happy ain't got nothing to do with it."

Jack walked past the doorman into the main entrance of the Hotel Monaco. He immediately had the distinct feeling that this was a place a man like him did not belong.

Then he caught sight of the person he was looking for.

The bellboy appeared to be in his mid-twenties; young enough that he would not have ascended the ranks of the hotel staff just yet, but old enough to have learned a thing or two. Jack stopped in front of him and pulled a twenty from his billfold.

"If I was going to have a secret meeting, where would I go?" Jack asked pointedly.

"What?" the bellboy asked.

Jack pressed the twenty into his hand.

"If I wanted to have a secret meeting with several of my friends, where would be the best place in this hotel to do something like that?"

"I—well, I guess the old ballroom."

"The old ballroom?" Jack asked.

"Yes, it's at the southern end of the hotel, past the last bank of elevators. It's been shut down for months for remodeling. No one goes there at this time of night, and no one will be there for hours. The night porter only comes around at six in the morning to do a grounds check."

. . .

"Do you remember the layout?" Eldred asked as they stood in the empty ballroom.

The Secret Service detail were surrounded by scaffolding, drop cloths, some painting equipment, and not much else. The ballroom of the Hotel Monaco had been chosen for this exact reason. It was historic enough to suit a meeting of such epic proportions but would also be completely private.

"Yes," Wilkins replied. He nodded toward the kitchen entrance. "Brezhnev and his men will enter through there."

"Good," Eldred said, turning to where Sid Felton stood at the rear entrance wearing his Stephen Lister mask. "Let's get the President in here."

Jack walked down the silent hallway and noted the elevators. He had reached the last bank. The entrance ahead of him would lead into the ballroom. This was it.

He drew his pistol from its holster and held it by his side. He did a quick check of the rest of his gear and then stepped forward. He paused again and listened.

There was definitely movement beyond the door ahead of him, but nothing that sounded obviously violent. As much as he hated to do it, Jack knew he had to wait for that. He needed to wait for the sound of obvious violence. If he broke into a legitimate meeting between the President of the United States and the Premier of the Soviet Union waving a gun around, all hell would let loose. He would most likely be shot down by the Secret Service before he made it two steps into the room.

Eldred stood and waited. Then, it happened. The kitchen door opened, and a man stepped out. He was obviously Soviet. Everything about him, from his manner of dress to the way he set his jaw, screamed it. He nodded, and Eldred nodded back. He reached out and waved a hand to Wilkins.

From out on the street came the sound of the sedan door opening and subsequent footsteps. Wilkins ushered the President inside, Sid Felton trailing close behind him.

The kitchen door opened again, and two more men exited. Behind them was Leonid Brezhnev, the Premier of the Soviet Union.

It's really him, Eldred thought to himself. He still couldn't believe this was happening.

.   .   .

There was a small sliver of a window in the door, and Jack stepped to it so that he could peer into the ballroom. Yes, there was the possibility that someone inside would see him, but that was a risk he had to take.

Holy shit, Jack thought to himself as he watched the President of the United States and the Soviet Premier shaking hands.

Then he saw something that made his blood run cold.

Stephen Lister was walking in the rear entrance.

Stephen Lister was dead.

The Apartment of Clark Finster
Langley, VA
March 21, 1981

"If you're who I think you are," Clark said, "you must know this stuff never works out. Come on... how many governments have you toppled?"

"Practice makes perfect," Vega said as he fixed a suppressor to his pistol. "Do you think da Vinci's first painting was a masterpiece?"

"Yes, it was the Baptism of Christ."

"Well, I don't know shit about art, but I do know a few things about murder. Like how to make this quick."

Vega pointed the suppressed pistol at Clark's head, and the analyst locked eyes with his would-be assassin.

"You're not going to close your eyes?" Vega asked quizzically. "Most people close their eyes."

"I'm not most people," Clark said.

Clark felt the zip of the round past his head and then watched as Vega stumbled backwards. Two more rounds hit him center mass, and he dropped to the floor.

"Down!" He heard Carrie's voice behind him.

Clark threw his body sideways, sending both him and the chair he was tied to crashing to the hardwood floor. Once he landed, he turned his head and stared into Vega's dead eyes.

Pryor had been going through Clark's desk for intelligence. He reacted when Carrie came barreling in the door, but not fast enough. The man went for the pistol he had carelessly placed on the desk and was answered by a round from Carrie's 1951 Beretta entering each of his knees. He fell to the floor, screaming.

Carrie walked over to him and put her boot on his chest.

She looked down at him.

"Quit your crying," she said, raising her pistol level with his chest. "No one gives a shit."

Carrie pulled her trigger twice and silenced the man's screams.

"He... might have known something," Clark said quietly.

"He didn't know anything," Carrie replied.

She pulled a knife from her belt and went to work on the binds securing Clark to the chair.

"Are you okay?" Carrie asked as she freed Clark's hands and he stumbled to his feet. She stared at him in shock. "Jesus. You don't look okay."

"What's wrong?" Clark asked.

Carrie looked down at the floor and then back to Clark.

"Don't move," Carrie said as she walked to the kitchen. "And whatever you do, don't look in a mirror."

Carrie rummaged through the kitchen until she found a large plastic bag and filled it with ice. She walked back to the living room, knelt down, picked something up from the floor, and dropped it into the sack. She then fixed a bandage to the side of Clark's head.

"What in the hell was that?" Clark asked as she finished her hasty first aid job.

Carrie looked him in the eyes.

"I'll tell you, but you can't freak out."

"I won't freak out," Clark said.

"It was your ear," Carrie said. "But they can probably put it back on."

"Okay," Clark said.

"I'm concerned about how well you're taking that news."

"I'm not freaking out," Clark said. "I'm pissed. There's a difference."

"Okay," Carrie said. "I can live with that. You're pissed. So, what are you going to do about it?"

Clark looked around for a moment as if trying to gather his thoughts.

"He said I was close," Clark said, walking over to his computer. "He said Tolya Rodin wouldn't be at his house—at Richard Feldman's house. He would be at some kind of secure location, waiting this thing out. That got me thinking about subterranean systems."

"Subterranean systems?"

Clark hit a few keys on the computer and a new screen popped up.

"Yes. I was running through his bank records earlier, and something jumped out at me. He uses a lot of power."

"I don't think that's a crime, Clark."

"No," Clark said as he stood back up. "He uses too much power for a house that size."

The Hotel Monaco
Washington D.C.
March 21, 1981

Jack did a quick survey of the ballroom, primarily because there was no time for anything more thorough. Stephen Lister/Sid Felton was quickly coming up on the group. There were two Secret Service men with the President and three guards with the Soviet Premier.

Jack knew the Secret Service protocols for an attack on the President. There was only one play to make. He pushed the door open, stepped into the room, raised his pistol, and fired a single round into the leg of the President of the United States.

Just as quickly, Jack pivoted back out the door and into the hallway, a split second before pistol rounds cracked around him, followed quickly by submachine gun fire. The protection detail had quickly transitioned to heavier artillery.

"Into the kitchen! Into the kitchen!" he heard one of the Secret Service men shouting.

Jack turned to see everyone frantically rushing through the small door to the kitchen, while Sid Felton very noticeably remained in the ballroom, looking confused. He had to be wondering what in the hell had just happened.

Jack drove his boot through the door and re-entered the ballroom, his weapon up and trained on Sid. The would-be assassin responded by drawing his own revolver. Jack fired twice, both rounds finding center mass and dropping Sid to the floor. Jack moved fast, kicking the gun away from the man and keeping his own pistol trained on him.

Sid looked into Jack's eyes.

"My old friend," Sid said lazily, a smile crossing his face. "I told you. I told you he'd be drawing flies soon."

"I thought you were talking about Reagan," Jack said. "Not Brezhnev."

"Doesn't matter," Sid replied. "They're all the same. Thought Police. I was trying to save you... trying to save all of you. Can't you see that?"

"It's over now," Jack said.

"Not yet," Sid said. "It's not over until I say it is."

Jack caught the movement out of the corner of his eye, and before his brain even registered what it was, he turned and sprinted away from Sid Felton. Sid had slipped a trigger device out of his shirt sleeve and into his hand.

There was only one possible reason for something like that.

Arkady felt the ground rumble beneath him and watched the windows at the back of the lower floor of the Hotel Monaco blow outward into the street. Alarm bells began to ring, and within moments, he saw people hurriedly exiting the building.

"What in the hell was that?" Richardson asked.

"That was the failsafe," Arkady replied. "We're going in."

"I have three men with me," Richardson said.

"Good men. We can handle whatever we meet, but..."

"What is it?" Arkady asked.

"Well, if the man inside detonated himself, what are the odds that anyone is left alive?"

Arkady surveyed this man coldly for a moment.

"My employer has much at stake in this venture," he said. "We cannot afford to play the game of 'what if.' Are you in this or not?"

"Of course," Richardson said quickly. He looked to where his men stood several feet away. "We're in it until it's done."

The Western Inn
Washington D.C.
March 21, 1981

Doctor Noah Barrister sat on the edge of the bed in the small motel room. He stared at himself in the dirty mirror hanging over the small dresser. He could not get over how old he looked. Or, at least, so he thought. The world had made him old.

He checked his watch and then nodded to

288 / JORDAN VEZINA

himself. It would be happening by now. Either Sid
Felton had killed the Soviet Premier, or Arkady
Radovich was leading the assault team to finish
the job.

The phone in the room rang.

Noah picked it up and put it to his ear.

He said nothing.

"We're going in," a voice on the other end said.

It was Richardson. He was a good man; another
of the Central America crew that had come over to
the hospital with Grunewald. Noah Barrister
thought back to those days. While he had high hopes
for this current venture with Tolya Rodin, he
wouldn't mind going back to the hospital setup.
That scenario had truly been the best of both
worlds. He received the respect due to him as a
medical professional while at the same time doing
the good work that was required to keep America
safe. At first, he had not liked the job, but now that it
was over, he had discovered a new appreciation
for it.

That appreciation was something his superiors at
the Agency had not understood when they had disci-
plined him after MK Ultra. This type of dark work
always had to be done by somebody, and it was unbe-
coming of a nation to throw those silent professionals

out with the garbage the moment the work was through.

That was the other problem: the perception that the work was through. The work was never through. That was something only Noah Barrister seemed to understand.

There was always work to be done.

There was a knock at the door.

Noah turned. He wasn't expecting any visitors.

He stood up quietly and scooped up the revolver that he had left on the dresser. In his stockinged feet, he moved carefully across the threadbare carpet to the door and peered through the peephole.

It was Grunewald. Noah let out a breath. He unlocked the door, and the big German walked in.

Grunewald closed the door.

"We're blown," he said. "It's over. We need to get out of here."

"What are you talking about?" Noah asked in confusion. "I just talked to Richardson. They're hitting the hotel as we speak."

"And why would they do that?" Grunewald asked pointedly. "Because Felton detonated?"

"Well... yes," Noah replied.

"It was Bonafide. He showed up at Lister's house."

"And bested you?" Noah asked with surprise.

"I'm man enough to admit when I'm outmatched. Jack Bonafide is something else, and we were not ready for him. Now, we have to run if we want to survive. I barely made it out of that house after he left. I practically had to tear my own hand off to escape the cuffs."

Noah looked down to Grunewald's left hand and saw that it was dripping with blood.

"I don't understand," Noah said.

Grunewald grabbed Noah by the shoulder and shook him.

"Listen to me!" he shouted. "There's no time for this! If we want this project to continue, we have to leave. *Now!*"

Noah Barrister thought for a moment and then nodded.

"I understand. Let me gather my things."

The Hotel Monaco
Washington D.C.
March 21, 1981

Jack sat up and blinked. The room was starting to come into focus, but his ears were ringing. He knew this wasn't an effect of his existing concussion symptoms, but as a result of the shockwave from the blast. He completed a quick pat-down and found he didn't have any holes in him. Not any new ones, at least.

He looked over his shoulder and saw what was left of Sid Felton. Doctor Barrister had done this to him, and Jack knew it. Just like he had probably been trying to do to him, too. Fortunately, Barrister hadn't understood just how resilient Jack's mind was.

Sid Felton, however, had been a different story.

Barrister was going to pay for this.

Jack stumbled to his feet and looked down to see the Colt 1911 still gripped in his right hand. *Son of a bitch.* He hadn't let it go, not even after being hit by the blast. That would be a good story to tell someone over a round of beers when he was an old man. One of many stories, assuming he made it that far.

There was a commotion in the kitchen, and Jack knew exactly what was going on. The Secret Service detail would have fallen back to an expedient safe room, which meant the walk-in freezer. They wouldn't have just charged out into the unknown. They would have Reagan and Brezhnev on ice—literally—while they radioed for back up.

"Drop it!" a voice called out.

Jack turned and couldn't believe his eyes.

It was Arkady Radovich.

Jack's pistol was still at his side. Was he fast enough? Was he faster than the former Alpha Group commander?

"I'm giving you a chance here, Jack," Arkady shouted. Four men walked in behind him, all heavily armed. "You don't have to die here. We only came for one man."

"Can't do that," Jack replied.

The kitchen door opened behind Jack, and Eldred Parks walked into the ballroom. He was a Texan like Jack and had seen combat on Iwo Jima as a young Private. Not much phased him. He had made a calculated decision that while this man had just shot the President in the leg, his threat status was outranked by the assault force that had just entered. Eldred held the submachine gun that had been stowed beneath his jacket at the ready.

"This is not a fight you want, friend," Arkady said. "We're not after the President."

"Don't matter much to me," Eldred said. "Both men are in my charge."

Jack turned to Eldred.

"I'm on your side," he said.

"No shit,' Eldred replied. "But your introductions need a little work."

"This isn't a fight you can win, Jack!" Arkady persisted.

"Winner takes all," Jack said.

Arkady cocked his head to the side.

"What are you talking about?"

Jack dropped his pistol to the floor, then reached behind his back and drew the Fairbairn-Sykes knife.

"What the hell do you think I mean?" Jack asked. "You may not have killed my brother, but you damn sure tried, and that counts for something."

Arkady stared at him for a moment. He stared at this mad American and then nodded. He wasn't sure what Jack Bonafide meant about his brother, because as far as Arkady knew Mac Bonafide was dead, but all the same, he dropped his rifle to the floor.

"Are you insane?" Richardson shouted from behind him. "We have a job to do!"

"And I'm doing it!" Arkady snapped. "The old-fashioned way."

He turned back to Jack, drew a knife from his belt, and stepped forward.

"Good luck," Eldred said.

"Don't need it," Jack replied.

An Undisclosed Location
Washington D.C.
March 21, 1981

Carrie pulled the car to a stop and turned to Clark.

"Are you sure you're okay?" she asked.

"I'm fine," Clark replied. "I just want to finish this."

Carrie looked out the windshield to the house ahead of them. It wasn't what she had expected. Yes, it was a nice enough house, but it didn't seem like the type of place that one of the wealthiest men in the world would live. It also didn't seem like the hardened residence of a rogue KGB agent in the midst of launching one of the most ambitious plots in the history of the world.

"This won't be easy," Clark said. "He won't just be sitting in the living room in an overstuffed chair."

"I figured as much," Carrie responded sarcastically. "So, where is he?"

"He'll be underground. We just have to figure out how to get to him."

Carrie moved around the side of the house with her pistol drawn. She looked for cameras and other security measures but found none. Ahead of her was the door. She reached out with her free hand and tested the handle.

It was unlocked. She looked over her shoulder at Clark, and he shrugged. They were in completely unknown territory.

Carrie opened the door and stepped inside.

The lights came on.

The Hotel Monaco
Washington D.C.
March 21, 1981

Jack lunged forward and caught Arkady on the right cheek with his blade. It was meant to be a stroke straight through his head, but the Russian was fast. He was much faster than even Jack had anticipated.

Arkady became lighter on his feet and smiled. He almost seemed to dance a little, as if, for once, he had not a care in the world.

"Men like us, Jack, we want a contest," Arkady said. "Isn't that right?"

"I didn't come here for small talk," Jack replied.

Jack feinted with his blade, then short-stepped forward and threw a hard kick to Arkady's shin. The Russian moved through the pain and slashed at Jack's three o'clock, drawing blood from his shoulder.

Jack moved as if the cut had not even happened and swung the handle of his knife hard into the side of Arkady's head. Jack didn't get the tunnel vision other men might in a situation like this, so he noticed that Arkady's men were poised to attack. It didn't really matter which way this fight went; they had no intention of backing down.

Jack had never believed either side would honor the so-called "terms" of this fight either way. It was just a delaying tactic, and they both knew it. The truth was that they had been in a stalemate. Both sides were too skilled, there was no cover, and they had nothing to lose. If they opened up on each other, most likely it would be a slaughter. At least this way Jack had some time to figure out what to do next. The only problem was that Arkady Radovich did as well.

Arkady stumbled, and it was clear that the strike from the handle of Jack's knife had hit home hard.

Again, Jack could see one of Arkady's men had his finger poised over the trigger of his carbine. He was ready to fire at any moment.

Jack felt the strike before he realized what had happened. He'd been distracted by trying to see everything at once, and instead had missed the only thing that mattered in that moment. He was treating Arkady like some sort of playground bully instead of the highly skilled operative that the man was. Now, Jack had paid for this mistake.

The bill came in the form of a chokeslam to the floor.

Arkady wound up for a hard overhand strike with his knife, and Jack responded by performing a quick turn of his hips, slapping a triangle choke on the big Russian and redirecting the force of the knife strike into Arkady's own leg.

Jack held Arkady's knife hand in place, using the pressure of the man's own arm to choke him out against the force of Jack's leg wrapped around his neck.

It was do-or-die time, and Jack knew it. There was no margin for error. He rolled onto his side with Arkady still in his grasp, drew his .38 from its ankle holster, and fired two shots in rapid succession, each one hitting the intended target.

"Don't do it!" Eldred shouted, lunging forward with his submachine gun toward the one remaining man.

Richardson froze. He wanted to get his MP5 up and take this man on, but in the confusion, the old Secret Service agent had gotten the drop on him, and they both knew it was over. If he tried to get his weapon on target, he would be dead before he even got his finger on the trigger.

Jack rolled one more time as Arkady's lights started to go out, and he put himself in the mount position, cranking down hard on the triangle choke. Arkady looked up at him, his eyes communicating a very clear message.

This is not over.

Arkady finally fell unconscious, and Jack relaxed his pressure to avoid killing him.

"Handcuffs!" Jack said, holding out his hand to Parks.

Eldred tossed a pair of steel handcuffs to him, and Jack rolled Arkady over and secured his hands behind his back. Without missing a beat, he sprang to his feet, snatched up his pistol, and moved on Richardson.

"Where's Barrister?"

"I don't know what you're talking about."

Jack lunged forward and slammed his 1911 into the side of Richardson's head, dropping the man to the floor.

"You have no time!" Jack said, pulling back the hammer on the pistol.

"You can't just kill him!" Eldred cut in.

"The hell I can't!"

"Wait!" Richardson said quickly. "If I talk, I want a deal!"

"You get to live," Jack said. "That sounds like a pretty good deal to me."

"I don't think so." Richardson sat up on the floor and looked around. "Sure, you can kill me, but if you do, you'll never find Doctor Barrister, and you'll never know how high up this really goes."

"I already know about Tolya Rodin," Jack said.

"You think that's where it ends?" Richardson scoffed. "Come on, Jack, use your head. You must know by now that we have the same employer."

"What in the hell is he talking about?" Eldred asked. "Jesus Christ! Are you both CIA?"

Jack looked at Eldred out of the corner of his eye but did not respond.

"Well, that fucking figures," Eldred said. "I swear you clowns cause far more trouble than you fix."

"And all you old men just want things to stay the same!" Richardson countered. "You sit around complaining that the world is going down the tubes, but you don't actually *do* anything about it! We're the ones doing what you won't!"

"By starting World War Three?" Eldred shot back.

"Enough!" Jack shouted. He turned and fired a single round into Richardson's right knee. "Talk!"

Richardson howled and grabbed at his leg. It was clear that any thoughts of further resistance had now vanished.

"No!" Eldred shouted. "You can't do that."

"Drop your weapon! Hands up!" Jack ordered, turning to Eldred with his Colt raised. "Do it! Now! I just shot the President of the United States. Don't test me."

Eldred looked Jack Bonafide in the eyes and took his measure. He knew that this man would do it. He knew he would kill him if he thought that it would bring him closer to accomplishing his mission.

"You're gonna burn for this," Eldred said as he dropped his gun. "This isn't how things are done."

"Be that as it may," Jack said, kicking Eldred's gun away, "this is what's happening. Cuff your hands behind your back."

"We can find another way to do this," Eldred said. He took out his spare handcuffs and hesitated before securing them. "I've got some pull. I can sort this out."

Jack pulled back the hammer on the Colt.

"I only speak one language," he said. "So, if you're not picking up what I'm laying down, we're in for a long night."

"Okay," Eldred said and secured his hands behind his back.

Jack turned his attention back to Richardson.

"You have three seconds. Three; two—"

"*The Western Inn!*" Richardson blurted. "That's where Barrister is!"

"Good," Jack said, and he headed for the door. "He and I have an ongoing disagreement about some lights."

"Wait!" Richardson shouted. "I need a tourniquet!"

"Need in one hand, shit in the other," Jack said coldly. "See which fills up first."

An Undisclosed Location
Washington D.C.
March 21, 1981

Clark froze. He didn't have his gun out. Why the hell hadn't he taken his gun out?

Carrie pivoted to the only figure she saw in the room. She had her gun out, and she trained the sights on Tolya Rodin as he stood up from his overstuffed chair beside the fireplace, both hands raised.

"I saw you coming," Tolya said. "On the closed-circuit television cameras."

"And this was your masterstroke?" Carrie asked. "To surrender?"

"No," Tolya said. "I am a painter whose master-stroke has yet to be made. May I sit back down?"

Carrie hesitated. The whole scenario had suddenly been turned on its ear. She had been expecting violence—a gunfight or an explosion, perhaps—but not this. Rodin was wearing a smoking jacket.

"I don't see why not," Carrie replied.

"You don't see why not?" Clark blurted. "He's a Soviet spy!"

"*Ex*-Soviet spy," Tolya corrected the analyst as he sat back down. "An ex-Soviet spy with bad hips."

Carrie lowered her weapon; not all the way, but enough to demonstrate a relaxed posture. She continued to scan the room, but it was becoming rapidly apparent that there was no one else besides Rodin.

"I can't see any other way this ends," Carrie said, "than us taking you in."

"That's where you're wrong," Tolya said. "I can see many possible futures. I can even see a future where you and I are working together."

Clark laughed out loud.

"You've got bad hips and a bad fucking brain!" he shouted. "You're the cause of all of this!"

"And what exactly, young man, is it that I am trying to do?"

"Start World War Three, for one!"

"A simple answer from a simple mind," Tolya replied.

"Fuck you!" Clark snapped. "How's that for simple?"

Carrie held up a hand.

"You're not buying into this, are you?" Clark asked.

Carrie turned and put a hand on Clark's chest.

"I need you to go outside," she said.

"What in the hell are you talking about?" Clark blurted. "This guy is Satan incarnate!"

"And you're letting your emotions control you. I

need to get him out of here without starting a fucking war. I can't do that if you're yelling at him."

"He's an old spy with bad hips! How is this a problem?"

"We have no idea who else he has here or what failsafes he can employ." Carrie narrowed her eyes at Clark. "You need to take a step back. You're not seeing this clearly. Wait outside."

Clark set his jaw for a moment and then nodded. He turned and walked back out the door they had entered through.

Carrie let out a breath and turned back to Tolya.

"Okay," she said. "Talk."

"Why are you here?" Tolya asked, and it was clear that this question had already been chambered and was ready to go.

"For you," Carrie replied. "I came here for you."

"Because I am the villain, correct?" Tolya asked. He stood up and walked across the room to the wet bar. "But beyond that, what is the end goal?"

"I don't understand the question."

Tolya stopped in the midst of preparing an Old Fashioned and looked at her.

"Don't you think that's a bit of a problem? Where is the finish line, Carrie? What is the end result you are hoping for?"

"To defend this country."

Tolya smiled and took a sip from his glass.

"A noble goal," he said. "Do you ever feel that you are alone in this pursuit?"

"This is boring," Carrie said. "Get to the point."

"True change comes from the barrel of a gun!" Tolya snapped, slamming his glass down on the countertop. "*You* should know that better than anyone. What is it you think we were trying to do with this attempt on the Premier? Please tell me you did not think it was something as simplistic as sparking World War Three. You're smarter than that."

"So, what was it?" Carrie asked. "You tell me, Rodin. What was the end goal?"

"*Progress.* The world as it stands right now is at a stalemate. Yes, there is a tentative 'peace,' if you even want to call it that, but true peace is achieved through fear of the inevitable."

"Which is what?" Carrie asked. "Armageddon?"

"A single superpower."

"Ah, I see," Carrie said. "And who wins in that coin toss?"

"Capitalism."

This took Carrie aback. It had not been the response she was expecting.

"What are you talking about?"

"Corporate rule, Carrie, is the only truly impartial form of governing a society. Consider this: wars are only fought on the stock exchange floor. The only casualties are the value of the dollar or the ruble and a depressed stock trader here and there. The people not only want this rule, but they will gladly line up for it and even pay for it."

"You're forgetting one thing," Carrie said.

"Which is?"

"Americans don't want to be ruled."

Tolya smiled and picked his drink back up.

"Of course they do," he said. "They just need that ruler to have a catchy jingle they can sing along to on the way to work. On the way to the very job where they will make the money they need to pay that ruler for his benevolent guidance."

"And I imagine that, in this equation, *you* are that ruler?"

"After a fashion," Tolya said, running his finger around the rim of his glass. "But the beauty of this idea is that the ruler doesn't matter. The *people* do. They make the decision for themselves with their dollar or their ruble. In this capitalist governance, we see true democracy. Not this battered whore the

Americans parade in front of the rest of the world as if it were the perfect system."

Shit, Carrie thought to herself. *He's making a lot of sense.*

"There's just one thing I don't understand," Carrie said.

"Which is?"

"Why are you telling me all of this?"

Tolya looked at her coldly for a moment and then smiled.

"Because, Carrie Davidson, every surgeon needs a scalpel."

"Maybe you were a better salesman back in Mother Russia, but I'm not buying it," Carrie said. "I'm still taking you in."

"To who?" Tolya asked as he walked back to his chair and picked up a file folder. He held it up to her, showing the seal of the Central Intelligence Agency emblazoned across the front. "To them?"

"Where did you get that?" Carrie asked.

"It doesn't matter so much where I got it," Tolya said, walking to her and holding out the folder, "but what it contains."

Carrie took the folder and opened it. It was her file; not the standard personnel jacket, but the CIA

Deep File on her that went far beyond what most Agency staff would ever see.

"I marked the pertinent sections for you," Tolya said, indicating the Post-it notes. "Makes for interesting reading. Particularly the part about using your neurological disorder as a screening tool for future black operations work."

Carrie read through the reports, her face blank. She had not been expecting this. This couldn't be true.

"All the way back to the orphanage," Tolya went on. "They knew then, because your father had it. Back in Czechoslovakia."

"This can't be true," Carrie said.

"But it is," Tolya said. "You were born to The Orphan Society, perhaps one of the greatest assassin mills in the history of the world. You were handpicked by Mother Marketa Dolak. I met her once during the course of my duties with Directorate S. A cold woman with a brutish soul and eyes deader than I have ever seen before or since."

"I was bought?" Carrie asked. She looked up at Tolya expectantly.

"Handpicked," Tolya corrected her. "But, yes, you were then purchased by the CIA and sent to live with your new family until such time as you would be gently nudged in the direction of becoming a CIA agent. Then, from there, well... you know the rest of that story."

Carrie closed the folder.

"My whole life is a lie."

"No," Tolya said. "Your whole life has been the only truth that matters. You were born, quite literally, for *this*, Carrie Davidson. You are the reaper. In the Orphan Society, there has always been one. One reaper. One who rises above all others and has the power to have a hand in shaping the world."

"What are you talking about?"

"My original offer is still very much on the table, Carrie. Become my reaper. Fulfill your destiny."

"I'm listening," Carrie said. "But first, I want to know more about this Orphan Society."

CHAPTER 9

**The Western Inn
Washington D.C.
March 21, 1981**

JACK BONAFIDE LOOKED across the street at the
Western Inn. He could feel a strange hesitation
clawing within him. He knew what it was: it was an
echo of everything that had happened to him inside
Saint Elizabeth's. It was an echo that refused to die.

He drew his Colt 1911 and did a brass check.
There was a round in the chamber, and he had a
full magazine. Most likely, he was just going up
against an unarmed old man. In the past, that

would have been a recipe for some flex cuffs or possibly even just a firm grip on the arm, but not this time. Jack knew how this equation was going to end.

"What are you going to do?" Angela asked.

"Settle a debt," Jack replied.

"When a man says something like that, it's never good."

Jack turned to her and stared through her. Angela could see that something wasn't right with him.

"Maybe men aren't ever good," Jack said. "Just less bad when it suits them."

Grunewald watched impatiently as Noah Barrister collected his belongings. The older man seemed to—in Grunewald's opinion—move exceptionally slowly. He thought for a moment about leaving him behind, but then dismissed the idea.

A man like Grunewald knew his strengths, but more importantly, he also understood his weaknesses. When it came to playing the heavy and getting the physical and tactical part of the job done, he had few peers. The genius of planning, though, was something that had always eluded him. It was a skill he did not possess, but fortunately for Grunewald, Doctor Noah Barrister did.

On account of things beginning to look like this job was not going to be a success, Grunewald would need a brain to do the planning for any future work. Despite the impending collapse of his current mission, he knew that Doctor Barrister was the right man to fill the bill.

It was also worth noting that Jack Bonafide had been a wild card. Bonafide was one of those men Grunewald had only encountered a few times in his career, but who he never forgot. He was the type of operative that every young man thinks he's going to be when he first joins the military or signs on with the CIA, although usually it doesn't work out that way.

Grunewald was good, no two ways about it. In fact, if he was setting his humility aside for just a moment, he would say he was probably one of the best in the world. Yet Jack Bonafide had put him away like a child putting away a toy. Perhaps that would have bothered another man at the German's level, but not Grunewald. Instead, it inspired him. He knew that men at Jack's level excelled, and he would keep pushing until he was one of them.

"Okay," Doctor Barrister said as he picked up his

bags. "I'm ready."

Grunewald leaned to the window and pushed the curtain aside.

"Shit," he said. "He's here."

"Are you sure?"

A .45 caliber round slammed through the paper-thin wall of the motel room and spun Grunewald like a top. He hit the floor, clutching his shoulder, already fishing for the tourniquet in his pocket with his wounded hand.

"Yes, I'm fucking *sure!*" Grunewald shouted as he commenced his hasty first aid.

This is no business for a psychiatrist, Noah Barrister thought as he stood staring at the single bullet hole in the wall. The light from the parking lot lamps shined through it onto his chest.

"Come out!" a voice called from outside.

Jack stood in the parking lot, Colt 1911 raised, two dozen feet from the entrance to the motel room. He had no intention of employing cover or any other tactics. Doctor Noah Barrister had gone after the bull, and now he was going to get the horns.

Jack figured there was someone else in the room, as the silhouette he had seen at the window was a

314 / JORDAN VEZINA

good deal larger than Barrister. It was pure guess-
work that the man would step to the center of the
room after he closed the curtains, but judging by the
scream that had followed Jack's single shot, that
guess had paid off.

The door to the room opened a crack, and then
opened fully. Framed in the doorway were Doctor
Barrister and Grunewald.

How in the hell had Grunewald made it from
the house all the way out here?

Jack could feel that his hand was shaking. The
moment he saw Doctor Barrister, he felt his blood
rise. The man had made him feel helpless. He had
pumped him full of drugs, toyed with his mind, and
forced him to kill people. Granted, they were all bad
men, but that still didn't make it right. Killing those
men should have been Jack's decision to make, and
no one had the right to take that choice away
from him.

He relaxed his grip on the pistol and tried to
control his breathing.

The two men fully emerged from the room and
closed the door behind them. They stopped on the
small sidewalk in front of the room, both looking
unsure as to what they should do next.

"Two fingers!" Jack shouted.

Grunewald held up his pistol with two fingers and tossed it across the parking lot. Part of him wanted to push his luck a bit, to see if he could go up against Jack and live to tell the tale, but the rational part of his mind made it clear to him that even if he might have been able to somehow get the upper hand with two arms, he was damn unlikely to pull it off with just one.

"You, too!" Jack ordered, turning his gun on Noah.

"I— I don't have a gun!" Noah stuttered. He had left the revolver in the hotel room.

"Well, that there is what we call in the business an 'error in judgement,'" Jack replied.

"I can disappear!" Grunewald blurted.

Jack stopped and turned his attention to the big German.

"I can disappear!" Grunewald repeated. "You know I can. We work for the same people. Think about it, Jack. What are you going to do? Shoot me? Arrest me? You arrest me, and I guarantee I'm back in some country in Central America toppling a government within a year. I'm too valuable to the government. I won't see a single day inside a cell."

Jack stared impassively at Grunewald.

"You know I'm right, Jack."

"You killed a Secret Service agent."

"I was doing my job!" Grunewald shouted.

"So am I," Jack replied.

Jack pulled the trigger and put a single round between Grunewald's eyes. The man's head whipped back in the darkness, and he hit the pavement with an audible thud.

"Jesus," Noah gasped. "You're a *monster*."

The words were calculated, and, this time, Jack was clear-headed enough to see the tactic for what it was. Doctor Noah Barrister was trying to control the situation; trying to control *him*.

Jack advanced on Noah.

"Who in the hell do you think you are?" Noah shouted.

This stopped Jack in his tracks. He felt the skin along his back go cold. It was the conditioning. It was still there.

"You heard me!" Noah pursued. "You fucking redneck! Who in the hell do you think you are? Don't you know who *I* am? I am a licensed medical doctor! Who are you? Some fucking redneck! If it weren't for that gun, you'd be stacking lumber in Texarkana right now."

"Shut up!" Jack shouted. "Shut your damn mouth!"

Noah took a step back. He had pushed too hard, and he knew it. This was a game of chess, and the penalty for losing was death.

"I understand," Noah said, raising his hands. "You want to be respected."

"I ain't buying it," Jack said. "So, you might as well stop trying to sell it."

Noah smiled.

"You remember me, don't you?"

"What?" Jack asked.

"Come on, Jack. I didn't recognize you until Grunewald brought me your file, and to be honest, you all kind of look the same to me. But I remember you from Selection. You remember, don't you?"

Everything suddenly clicked into place. During the initial development phase of Selection for Delta Force, Colonel Charlie Beckwith had brought in a psychiatrist to test the mental fortitude of the men. This psychiatrist had been on loan from the CIA, and he had taken things too far. Jack remembered this man asking him obscene questions, calling him a "redneck," and, somehow, he had even known all about Jack's uncle, John Bonafide. This man had told Jack that he was just like his Uncle, and he would also kill women and children, given half the chance.

"I thought so," Noah continued. "So, you

remember that I was trying to help you, all the way back then. Just like I was trying to help you in the hospital. You see, Jack; that's the thing with being sick. Sometimes you don't even know you have a problem. That's why men like me exist; to help men like you heal. To help you understand who it is you're supposed to be."

For just a moment, Jack felt his mind starting to give way. He felt himself starting to wonder if this man was right; if perhaps he had *always* been right about him.

Then the ringing in his ears started. This time, it was different, almost as if it were a clarion call punching a hole through the darkness, cutting through the white noise of Doctor Noah Barrister's tricks. Jack's heart rate went through the roof, and his chest tightened. They were the old heart attack symptoms, but again, this time they were different. They narrowed his focus down to a laser's sharpness.

Jack raised his weapon again and Noah stepped back, this time all the way against the wall. He could see in Jack's eyes that his gambit had failed. He wasn't going to talk his way out of this one, but still he would try.

"Come on, Jack. There's something you want to tell me, isn't there? Something that's been eating you up inside? Something you want to confess, to feel whole again?"

"Yes," Jack said. "There is."

"Tell me, Jack. You can tell me anything."

Jack Bonafide drove his gun forward and fired five rounds into Doctor Noah Barrister. They ripped through the man's body and left him wide-eyed with his mouth open as he slid down the wall to the sidewalk, leaving a trail of blood behind him.

Jack took a few steps forward and looked down at the body of Doctor Barrister.

"I see two lights, you son of a bitch."

An Undisclosed Location
Washington D.C.
March 21, 1981

Clark stood in the cold and darkness outside the house. He had been watching the conversation between Carrie and Tolya with great interest. It was insane; they should have been dragging this man away in handcuffs, not listening to him make his sales pitch for a global government.

Something had been gnawing at Clark for a while, all the way back to New York, when they had taken down that "white power" encampment upstate. That was the first time he had started to think that there might be something wrong with Carrie. The question was if it was serious enough to file some sort of a report on her.

The reason he hadn't taken action was that there was something wrong with *all of them*, him and Jack included. You didn't get to their level within the CIA without having a few screws loose. It was just a matter of whether there were enough loose screws to bring the whole house down.

"Please don't try to be a hero," Carrie said from behind Clark.

He didn't move a muscle. She had somehow exited the house and come up behind him in the darkness.

"I've been accused of a lot of things," Clark said. "But being a hero isn't one of them."

"Raise your hands," Carrie ordered.

Clark did as he was told and felt Carrie reach around from behind him into his jacket and pull his pistol out of its holster. She threw it away into the yard.

"What are you doing, Carrie?" Clark asked, turning around to face her, careful to move slowly.

"I have to play this out," Carrie said. "What Rodin's saying makes sense to me. It makes a lot more sense than what we've been doing."

"Please, Carrie. You don't even have to bring him in. Just come with me. We'll find some people that can help you."

Clark instantly knew he had chosen his words poorly.

Carrie's face twisted in anger.

"Help me?" she snapped. "Who in the hell do you think you are? I'm not the one who needs help here!"

Carrie raised her pistol at a canted angle and pointed it at Clark's head.

"Tell me, Clark! Do I need help?"

"No! I'm sorry! I didn't mean anything by it!"

"We almost let a fucking hydrogen bomb go off in New York, and then we almost let a nuclear power plant melt down! How is that a good track record?"

"You know we weren't the cause of that."

"What has Rodin done, Clark? We're going to haul him into the CIA, where he'll either disappear down a black hole or be executed, and for what?"

"He staged a plot to execute the Soviet Premier."

"Think about what you just said! He staged a plot to kill the sworn enemy of our country! He had the balls to do what none of us could!"

Clark said nothing. He knew that she was beyond reason. Some contact in her mind had broken. She was somewhere else now.

"Put your hands behind your back," Carrie said.

"No," Clark replied. "We're going to come after you. You must know that."

"I know," Carrie said as she slammed the butt of her pistol into the side of Clark's head.

The Western Inn
Washington D.C.
March 21, 1981

Jack Bonafide stood staring at the body of Doctor Noah Barrister in the parking lot. His eyes were wet. He could feel it, but he didn't think he was crying. He couldn't seem to break out of the trance he was in.

In the distance, he heard sirens, and he knew that they were coming for him. Someone would have called the gunshots in by now. How long had he been standing there? He had no idea. He needed to move, but he just couldn't.

"Jack?" a woman's voice asked softly from behind him.

It was reflex, nothing more. Jack turned on a dime and brought his Colt 1911 up to acquire his target. It was reflex, nothing more.

Angela Merril's breath caught in her throat, and she raised her hands.

"Jack, no!" she pleaded. "It's me!"

Jack held his weapon up for a moment longer and then lowered it. After a few more seconds, he relaxed fully and holstered the pistol.

Angela looked from Jack to the bodies of Grunewald and Noah Barrister.

"My God," she said quietly. "They're dead."

"They had it coming," Jack replied, and he walked past her toward the car. He stopped when he realized she wasn't following him and turned to her. "What's wrong?"

"I don't do this, Jack!" she shouted. "This isn't how I want my life to be!"

"The police are coming," Jack said calmly. "We have to go."

"I thought you were with the police? I thought you were CIA or something."

"I am, but the CIA and the police don't always agree on the finer points of the law. We can't be here when they arrive."

"I'm not going," Angela said flatly. "I'm staying here."

"Then they'll arrest you."

"I'll take my chances."

Jack looked down the road toward the sound of the sirens that were getting ever closer.

"That's not an option," he said. "You need to come with me."

"Or what?" Angela countered. "Will you shoot me, too?"

"It's not like that," Jack said. "You don't know what those two did."

"To you?" Angela asked.

"Now isn't the time to talk about it."

Angela walked forward to Jack and took his hand in hers. She looked up into his eyes.

"Will there be a time, Jack?"

He closed his hand a little tighter around hers.

"Yes."

"Okay," Angela said. "In that case, I'll go with you."

Los Angeles, CA
March 21, 1981

Assistant Director of the CIA Michael Scarn rubbed his eyes as he sat in the back of the cab that was taking him to the CIA safehouse. Of course, the driver had no idea where he was going or what Michael Scarn's business in Los Angeles was. If he did, he would most likely change his course of travel and get as far away from the city as possible.

The phone inside Scarn's suitcase beeped, and he dipped into it to retrieve the large mobile phone.

"That one of those cellular phones?" the driver asked.

"Wave of the future," Scarn said, hitting the button to accept the call.

"I don't know," the driver replied. "I like being at home when I talk on the phone."

"This is Scarn."

"Scarn, this is Tresham."

Scarn sat up a little straighter in his seat. "Yes, sir."

"Barrister is dead, and Reagan's been shot."

"What?" Scarn blurted.

"That's not the half of it," Tresham replied. "Don't worry, the President is fine. He's getting out of surgery now. Just a leg wound. Barrister, though— he won't be accepting any dinner invitations anytime soon."

"What about Jack and the rest of the group?"

"That's a long fucking story," Tresham groused. "They're mostly fine, but it looks like Carrie might have thrown in her lot with Tolya Rodin."

"What?" Scarn nearly shouted. It was enough to catch the driver's attention.

"We don't have anything concrete yet, but Clark thinks it may have something to do with Carrie's brain condition. She may not be right in the head."

"This is a big problem, Mike. That woman is dangerous."

"Agreed," Tresham said. "But we have a bigger problem. Intelligence just came through that East Germany may have a covert in place to use that anthrax shipment you're after."

Scarn felt his breath catch in his throat. "You're serious."

"Yes," Tresham replied. "Your task just got a whole lot more urgent."

"Should we be bringing more people in on this?"

"We already have a damn team on site!" Tresham snapped, and then he paused for a moment to collect himself. "That's why you're en route, Scarn. To figure out what the hell is going on. We shouldn't need to bring more people into a situation like this. And even if we wanted to, there just isn't enough actionable intelligence."

"Story of my life," Scarn groused.

"Ours is not to question why," Tresham said.

"I'm not a fan of how that saying ends," Scarn countered.

"Then don't fail," Tresham replied.

"This is an unusual request," the page said as he looked over the package that Wilhelm Fischer had handed him. "You want me to wait to hand this to the news desk?"

Wilhelm peeled off another hundred-dollar bill and held it out to the page. "Yes, and if you do this right, I'll be back with another of these."

The page was obviously suspicious of this whole scenario, but he was also being offered more money than he made in a week to do a few minutes of work.

"Okay," the page said with a shrug, shoving the VHS tape into his jacket pocket. "I'll deliver it to the news desk at noon."

"Excellent," Wilhelm said with a smile.

He waited as the page re-entered the building and then turned to where the Paul Hastings Tower stood several blocks away. He wondered if the newscasters would be alive long enough to deliver his message.

Scarn stopped in front of the unassuming building and looked up to the closed-circuit camera that was mounted above what was almost certainly a steel re-enforced door. He thought to himself that they needed to find a way to conceal those cameras. There wasn't much point in having a safehouse if there was a virtual flag waving in front of it to let everyone know it was some sort of a hardened building.

The door buzzed, and there was an audible

unlocking sound. Scarn stepped forward and pushed it open. Inside the main entryway, he found the lead agent, Pritchard Jones. He looked just as Scarn remembered him from the Academy. Jones wore a ready smile and thrust his hand out.

"Assistant Director Scarn," Jones said. "I'm Supervisory Special Agent—"

"I know who you are," Scarn said. "Have you been updated by the Director?"

Jones looked confused. "Updated? On what?"

"Jesus Christ, man!" Scarn snapped. "We have an actionable threat on the biological contaminate you're tracking!"

"We do?"

A voice called out from the next room. "He's right! The message just came through!"

Jones turned on a dime. His demeanor completely changed, and he hurried back into the main room. Scarn felt better; it was obvious the man wasn't some smiling clown who had just bumbled his way into this position.

"What is it?" Jones asked.

"Hold on," the agent said, holding up a hand. "There's more coming through."

The room waited in silence as the agent read the dispatch and then looked up at Scarn.

"It says we should be on the lookout for someone named Wilhelm Fischer?"

"*Jesus,*" Scarn gasped.

"I take it that name means something to you?" Jones asked.

"This is real," Scarn said. "We have to find that man and we need to lock down that anthrax."

CHAPTER 10

CIA Headquarters
Langley, Virginia
March 23, 1981

JACK BONAFIDE LOOKED around the White Room they were sitting in and felt as if he were waiting for the hammer to fall. Secret Service Supervisory Agent Eldred Parks sat at one end of the room with a thin file folder on one knee and a scowl on his face. It was no big mystery that Eldred had not cared for how Jack had handled the attempt on the Soviet Premier, and it showed. This was to say nothing of the fact that Jack had backed the man down at gunpoint and then handcuffed him.

That being said, even Eldred could not argue with the outcome. Both the Premier and President Reagan were still alive, albeit the former with a slight limp. A story would be floated to the media that the President had twisted his knee getting down from a horse at his ranch. No one would ever know he had been shot, and they would certainly never know that it had been by one of his own intelligence agents.

Beside Jack sat Clark Finster. The young man had a bandage on his head from where he had taken a nasty blow, and another from where his ear had apparently been re-attached, but that was all Jack knew about what Clark had been through. Following the events at the Hotel Monaco, they had all been placed in quarantine upon their arrival at Headquarters, in order to get everyone's story without external influence.

The door to the room opened, and Director of the CIA Mike Tresham stepped in. He shut the door behind him.

"Well, holy shit!" Tresham nearly shouted. "This is quite a little circus we have going here."

No one replied.

Tresham turned to Eldred Parks.

"What's your status on this thing? Is my man going to federal prison?"

Eldred waited for a moment and then answered.

"No, Director. In fact, the President has asked me to extend his personal gratitude to Agent Bonafide for his actions at the Hotel Monaco, although he will be forwarding his surgical bill."

No one laughed.

"And what you?" Tresham asked. "Where do you stand on this?"

"I don't understand the question, sir," Eldred replied.

"You're the ranking agent on the President's detail. Your opinion matters."

Eldred seemed to study the question for a moment and then finally let out a sigh.

"I don't like how it was handled," he responded. "And I sure don't like that your man shot the President or the way he handled the opposition force."

Eldred paused again. It was clear that he did not intend to get in a pissing contest over Jack threatening his life. "That being said, if I'm being honest about it, I can't say I could have done it any better."

"Agreed," Tresham said. He turned to Jack. "So, looks like you're off the hook, Bonafide. *Again.* I'm surprised you can even sit in that chair with the size of the horseshoe that must be shoved up your ass."

Jack allowed himself a smile, but he had been working for Mike Tresham long enough to know that he was far from off the hook.

"You murdered those men at the Western Inn," Tresham pressed. "Just so we're clear on that. I get why you did it; I know what they did to you. But it can't happen again. You have to be better than that. *We* have to be better than that."

"Understood," Jack replied.

Mike Tresham turned to Clark.

"I know you're on top of Carrie's new status as an enemy agent and you haven't slept in three days, but what have you got?"

"She's gone rogue," Clark confirmed.

This was the first Jack had heard of Carrie's situation.

"What do you mean 'rogue?'" he asked.

"She's thrown her lot in with Tolya Rodin," Clark replied.

"There's no way," Jack said quickly. "She's trying to get leverage on him, work undercover."

"Jack... she's not," Clark said with a shake of his head. "It's that brain thing she has. It's changed her. I started noticing it from the way she was going after Kelvin."

"Kelvin is a piece of garbage," Jack shot back.

"I get it," Clark said. "I do. But still... The way she was acting, it was clear something was off. She came back to my place after you left. Some of Barrister's men were trying to get me to talk. She came out of nowhere and executed them."

"Good. That's her job."

"Not like that," Clark said. "You weren't there. You didn't see the look in her eyes. She *enjoyed* it."

Jack wanted to counter again; to push back against the idea that this woman he had been depending on since the hunt for the Black Tsar had suddenly broken bad, but he also knew Clark wouldn't make up something like this.

"Okay," Jack said. "What are we doing about it?"

"We have to find her so that we can bring her in and get her the help she needs," Clark said.

Mike Tresham and Clark exchanged a look that Jack did not miss.

Jack stood up out of his chair and moved aggressively toward Tresham, in a way the Director had never seen him move before.

"I've got a fucking chit!" Jack shouted. "After everything I've been through, I've got a chit with the

Agency and with you, and I'm cashing it in. It's a capture mission, flat out!"

Mike Tresham said nothing.

"That's the only way this works, Mike. If you can't do it that way, I walk."

"You have my word," Tresham said. "Capture only."

The door to the White Room opened, and a red light came on, alerting everyone inside that it was no longer secure. At the door was a senior analyst whose name Mike Tresham could not remember.

"What the fuck are you doing?" Tresham shouted, as breaking the seal of a White Room during a debrief was expressly forbidden.

"Sir, you need to come with me now. We're going to a safe location."

Tresham looked beyond the analyst to the group of heavily armed men rapidly approaching.

"What's happened?"

"Jesus Christ!" Clark gasped as the men stood in the Operations Center.

Mike Tresham had refused to be whisked away to a 'safe location,' instead opting to stay on site with a heavily armed escort.

"How many?" Jack asked as he watched the news reports coming through.

"Three hundred dead," the analyst said. "We don't know how many have been infected. We're co-ordinating with the meteorological service and Fort Meade to start building a damage model on what we're dealing with."

"What's the worst-case scenario?" Tresham asked.

The analyst became stone-faced.

"Shit," Tresham groused.

"The problem is that once a person is infected with anthrax, it can take up to two months for them to expire. We have no way of performing mass testing, and we have no way of knowing exactly how many are infected. California National Guard is preparing to mobilize. They're just waiting on word from the Governor, but that should be coming any minute."

"Sir!" another analyst shouted. He was running toward Tresham and holding up a phone. "It's the Assistant Director!"

Tresham snatched the phone and put it next to his ear.

"Scarn! Where in the hell are you?"

"Mister... Tresham... I'm on the roof of the Paul

Hastings Tower," Scarn said. His breathing was obviously labored. "I've just killed Wilhelm Fischer."

"Holy shit!" Tresham shouted. "At least we got the son of a bitch. I need you to get back here ASAP to help me co-ordinate a response."

"I don't think that's a good idea," Scarn said. "The vial was on a timer. It went off after I killed him. I'm infected."

"You can't know that," Tresham said.

"I know it!" Scarn said firmly. "Trust me, sir. There's no point in me trying to come back there. I'm more use on the ground here."

"What aren't you telling me?" Tresham asked.

"When I searched Fischer, I found a map with two other locations marked off. There may be two more vials out there. I'm going after them."

Tresham hesitated and then let out a breath.

"Scarn, when we met, I thought you were a bit of a princess," he said. "I'm glad I was wrong about that."

"Thank you, sir."

"Go find those vials before more people die."

"Yes, sir. It was an honor working with you."

"I—" Tresham started to say something but couldn't find the words.

Scarn took care of it for him by ending the call.

Mike Tresham stared at the phone for a moment and then looked at Jack.

"I assume you heard all that?" he asked.

"Yes, sir."

"What's your priority right now?"

"You just tell me what you need," Jack said. "I'm in this for the duration."

Jack downed the black coffee like a shot, and Clark winced as he observed the display.

"Doesn't that burn your throat?" Clark asked.

"Can't feel heat anymore," Jack replied. "Not since the hospital. Just feels like... I don't know. Feels dull. Numb."

"You might want to get that checked out."

"That's the least of my problems."

Jack thought about Angela Merril and how he had handed her off to an emergency response team when he had returned to Langley. There was no other option, but he still hated doing it. She had been there for him when he'd needed her most; not just once, but twice now. He knew she would be okay, but he felt like he owed her more than that.

He had already started to wonder if there was

something more between them than just a caregiver/patient relationship.

The door to Director Tresham's door opened, and the man himself waved them inside.

Jack checked his watch. It had been just under three hours since the attack on Los Angeles.

Jack and Clark walked into the office, and then Jack saw something that stopped dead him in his tracks.

"*Well*," Jack said with a smile. "I'll be a son of a bitch."

"Your words," Will Hessler said as he stepped forward and shook Jack's hand. "Not mine."

"I never thought I'd see you again," Jack said. "Not after that number you did on the KGB."

"The KGB?" Clark asked.

"Yes," Mike Tresham said. "Our friend here is the one who took down the KGB back in February."

"That was *you?*" Clark asked. "You're Jericho Black?"

"I had help," Will replied sheepishly. It was clear that he was uncomfortable receiving the credit for the operation that had effectively dismantled the Soviet Union's premier intelligence agency.

Clark knew he shouldn't be so surprised, but

when it came to Jericho Black, he had been expecting someone a little more like Jack. He had followed all the intelligence reports on Jericho Black, not just those during the KGB operation but all the way back to the first days he had surfaced within Israeli Intelligence. The man he had read about had seemed larger than life, like some kind of unstoppable Jewish superman.

The first thing that struck Clark was that this man was clearly *not* Jewish. The files had reported that Black had gone to Israel from the United States, but even so, he had assumed that the man would be Jewish.

He also thought that he would be older.

Will Hessler was the picture of the blue-eyed, blond-haired all-American boy. Not only that, but he was young. He couldn't have been much older than Clark.

"What are you doing here?" Jack asked.

Will looked to Mike Tresham who gave him a nod.

"I work for the Agency," he said. "On a contractual basis."

Jack was surprised.

"For how long?" he asked.

"Not long," Will replied. "In fact, I was getting

ready to give Mister Tresham my final walking papers when I saw the news come through this morning."

Jack turned to Tresham.

"What's the play?"

"There is no play," Tresham said. "At least, not one that can undo what's been done. That toothpaste is out of the tube, and it's fucking anthrax-flavored."

"Scarn?" Jack asked.

"He's dark. He has reason to believe there are two more terror cells linked to Wilhelm Fischer, and he's trying to take them down before anyone else dies."

Jack looked down at the floor.

"I could have stopped it," he said. "If I'd been faster in New York. If I'd caught up to him sooner."

Tresham grabbed Jack by the shoulder and shook him.

"Knock it off!" the Director snapped. "We can't turn back time, and we can't waste what little time we have playing Monday morning quarterback. We have to take action now."

"You said you needed me to help Jack with a job," Will said.

This caught Jack's attention. He met Tresham's eyes.

"What job?"

Tresham held Jack's gaze for a moment.

"We can't put the toothpaste back in the tube," Tresham said. "But we can sure as hell murder the son of a bitch who squeezed it out."

Jack looked over the makeshift Ops board that had been assembled in the Director's office; a board that would be incinerated once Will Hessler had finished committing it to memory. Jack remembered that the man had some kind of photographic memory. If they actually carried out this job, that would certainly come in handy.

"It's a suicide mission," Clark said.

"It's *not* a suicide mission," Tresham insisted. "Admittedly, the odds of survival aren't great, but survival isn't the point."

"*Payback*," Jack said. "Right?"

"Plain and simple," Tresham said. "We can't prove it conclusively and no one will ever green-light the investigation to prove it, but we know this Heinrich Weber was the one who set Wilhelm Fischer on his path. We also know there's some money man out there linked to Weber, but we haven't uncovered him yet. Clark, that's your job."

344 / JORDAN VEZINA

"I'll find him," Clark said.

"Will," Tresham continued. "You and Weber have a history."

Will nodded.

"Even before I knew he existed, he was tied up in everything that happened to me. I already had a score to settle with him. This just seals the deal."

Jack continued to scan the board. It was covered with photos of known subjects within East German Intelligence and maps of East Berlin and Leipzig. Clark was right. On paper, it was a suicide mission, but in his mind's eye, Jack Bonafide could see another version. He could do this. He knew he could.

"We can pull it off," Jack said, before turning to Will. "Do you think we can?"

Will looked to the Ops board and then back to Jack.

"I HALO-jumped into the middle of the Siberian forest, rode a train to Moscow, got in a street fight with a bunch of former Soviet Special Forces soldiers, and then blew the shit out of the KGB. I can do this job without even spilling the tequila out of my glass."

Tresham laughed.

"Well, I'm glad you're confident, but don't get

cocky," he said. "Yes, I want my pound of flesh, but I also want you two back here alive."

"What kind of assets do we have on the ground?" Jack asked.

"We've had an Alpha Team there since the beginning."

"I heard about that," Jack said. "I was just never sure if it was true."

"We kept it under wraps as best we could," Tresham said. "But we've had Army Special Forces operating in Eastern Europe for decades with a cover so thin you can see through it."

"Why do the East Germans allow it?" Will asked.

"Go along to get along," Tresham said with a shrug. "They do the same thing to us; we're just better at it. Of course, I'm biased."

"We have a contact on the ground?" Jack asked.

"A Special Forces Major named Randall. Mick Randall. He's been running photo surveillance all over East Germany for eighteen months now. He was supposed to have been rotated out, but I put a stop order on that. You'll be meeting him on the other side of the Wall."

"Then what?" Will asked.

346 / JORDAN VEZINA

"Find Weber and bring me his head," Tresham said bluntly.

Will smiled.

"Will do. One dead East German coming up."

Tresham stood up a little straighter, and his face became somehow more menacing.

"I just want to ensure, young man, that you understand what I'm saying. I am not speaking figuratively," Tresham continued. "I am speaking *literally*. I want you back here with that Kraut's head in a sack."

**Gare du Palais Train Station
Quebec City, Quebec
March 24, 1981**

Daniel Flynn scanned the Arrivals board from across the train station and found her target. Outside, dawn had already broken, and she could feel the warmth of the sun on her face. She knew that it would soon start making her eyes hurt, so she slipped on her sunglasses.

She reached down, tapped the Ruger secured in her waistband, and scanned the train station again. Just the normal crowd of morning commuters.

Both Mac Bonafide and the Russian, Yahontov, would be with Kelvin. Neither of them would be a problem. If it was David Kelvin they were accompanying, there was a good chance the man would try to make a break for it, for which she would be perfectly happy to put a bullet in him right in the middle of the crowded train station.

The attack on Los Angeles had already happened. There was no undoing that, but she could, at least, get her pound of flesh.

If it was Dave Kelvin, on the other hand, she would need to keep her head on a swivel. That one would not go down quite as easily as his weaker half.

The obvious question was: then what?

Daniel Flynn knew perfectly well what was coming: the darkness. This new Director of the CIA sounded like one of those Boy Scouts who would dismantle her unit, such as it was. Kelvin would be dead. In essence, her work would be finished. Which meant that *she* would be, as well.

Daniel Flynn would most likely check herself into a cheap motel, drain a bottle of equally cheap whiskey, and then eat her own gun. She had always known that was how it would end for her, all the way back to the beginning of it all in Denmark. It had been like a portent of doom hanging over her head; a dark angel escorting her through the years, always breathing its acrid stench across the back of her neck.

A loud dinging filled the station, snapping Daniel out of her thoughts. She watched the train roll to a stop, and within moments, the passengers began disembarking. She rested her hand on the butt of her pistol, not caring who saw it.

This was it. This was the end.

"If you're looking for me," Dave Kelvin said, "you're facing the wrong direction."

Daniel didn't move, because she could feel the gun pressed against her back.

"I assume I'm not talking to David," Flynn said.

"No. What tipped you off? That I don't sound like a girl?" Dave Kelvin sneered. "Let's go."

Kelvin grabbed Daniel by the shoulder and lead her across the platform.

"The gun," Kelvin said. "Ditch it under the train."

Daniel did as she was instructed. She knew when she was outmatched, and this, unavoidably, was one of those times. She looked around, thinking someone might have seen her toss a pistol beneath the train, but no such luck.

"Through that door," Kelvin said, nodding to an exit in front of them.

Daniel pushed it open, and they exited to the side of the building. The sun rose on the opposite side of the station, so the exterior of the building was still soaked in semi-darkness.

"Stop!" Kelvin ordered.

Daniel complied and turned to face him. He was just as she remembered him.

"What now?" Daniel asked. "You're just going to shoot me?"

"Isn't that what you were going to do to me?" Kelvin asked. "Hell, isn't that what you sent Bonafide and the skirt to do? Murder me?"

"I don't know if 'murder' is quite the word I would use," Daniel countered. "More like *retribution*."

"You're still wound up about the teeth, aren't you?" Kelvin asked.

"Twenty million dollars in Nazi gold, you son of a bitch, and all of it in teeth pulled from dead Jews in the camps! How in the hell do you sleep at night?"

"Chamomile tea and a night mask," Kelvin mocked.

"You're going to burn for what you did," Daniel pressed on. "I'm not the only one who has a score to settle with you."

"Oh, really?" Kelvin asked. "And who, pray tell, should have me shaking in my boots at the very thought of them coming after me?"

"The Orphan Society."

Kelvin's face changed. The sneer was gone.

"I thought that would get your attention," Flynn said.

"Impossible. Even if you could afford it, they would never take the job."

"They've already taken it," Daniel replied. "And as for the money, cheap whiskey doesn't cost much, and the government covers my food and board. I've been socking it away for years. Now, I have a dead man's switch set up with your name on it. So, you can kill me if you want, but then you might as well kill yourself. Because they're coming for you."

Kelvin took a step back.

"Are you turning chickenshit?" Daniel asked.

"The rules of the game just changed," Kelvin said. "But this isn't over."

Daniel stared at him.

"That's where you're wrong, Dave," she said, and in one fluid movement, she raised her leg and pulled a .38 Special from an ankle holster. She put the gun to her own head. "I make the rules."

Daniel pulled the trigger. Her blood spattered the wall behind her and to the left, and then her body crumpled to the ground.

"Shit," Kelvin said quietly.

The Apartment of Angela Merril
Washington D.C.
April 2, 1981

Angela Merril walked across her dark apartment and took a half-kneeling position in front of her phone. She gently tapped the light that would indicate a message on her machine, but she knew there was nothing wrong with it.

The reality was that no one had called. Specifically, Jack Bonafide had not called. She thought back to the way he had squeezed her hand in the parking lot of the Western Inn. She had thought that meant something. He had even told her that it did. He had told her they would talk about what he was feeling.

"Promises are important," Angela said to herself.

She stood back up and walked to the stool in front of her kitchen counter. She sat down on it and looked at the objects neatly lined up. First was the sterilized towel with three scalpels. Beside those was her termination letter from the Bethesda Naval Hospital, along with the letter informing her that she would no longer qualify for government work in her field of specialty.

The last object on the counter was the bottle of Haldol, the medication that helped her to manage her schizophrenia. *If* she even really had it, which she highly doubted. She only took the medication because she had made a promise a long time ago that she would.

After Jack had dropped her like a bag of garbage at Langley, the agents had debriefed her and taken her statement. Then they had done their normal due diligence, which included an exhaustive background check. Exhaustive enough to uncover Angela's psychiatric history; the one she had managed to keep hidden for so long.

The one that would have stayed hidden, had it not been for Jack.

Angela reached across the counter, unscrewed the top of the bottle of alcohol, and then used it to soak a cotton pad to sterilize the scalpels again. This would be the fifth time. They would never be clean enough. Not for this kind of work.

She pulled back her robe to reveal the flesh of her right thigh, picked up the first scalpel, and began drawing a line across her flesh, a flow of blood following. She bit her lip and felt the tears beginning to flow.

"I hate you. I hate you. I hate you," she cried, until the blade had finished its journey. She quickly dropped the scalpel with a clatter and snatched up some gauze to cover the wound.

The crying turned to deep, rolling sobs which spilt from the depths of her wounded heart.

She looked at herself in the mirror and repeated the mantra.

"I hate you. I hate you. I hate you."

Finally, Angela stopped crying and reached once more to the counter. She slid a photo toward her and looked down at it. It was a photo of Jack that she had taken from his patient file at Bethesda.

"But I hate *you* most of all, Jack Bonafide."

The story continues in
Jack Bonafide Book 4: Counter Assault

Coming soon to Amazon!

Did you enjoy Breakdown? Please consider
providing a review on Amazon. Your reviews keep
these books coming!

Review Breakdown!

ABOUT THE AUTHOR

Jordan Vezina is a fiction writer living in Austin, Texas with his wife Emily where they run a business together. Jordan served in both the Marine Corps and Army Infantry, and worked as a bodyguard. This background provided much of the detail regarding weapons and tactics in the Jericho Black and Jack Bonafide books.

The Jericho Black Universe contains the Jericho Black, Jacob Mitzak and Jack Bonafide series of books.

Make sure to subscribe and follow using the links below for updates on new releases

jordanvezina.com
hello@jordanvezina.com

Printed in Great Britain
by Amazon